12/02.

HOW TO BE A REAL PERSON

(in just one day)

Sally Warner

Alfred A. Knopf · New York

To my editor, Tracy Gates,
who has brought out the best in me,

and to my friend Fred Green,
who told me a story one afternoon....

I also thank Scott O'Dell, of course, for writing
the wonderful *Island of the Blue Dolphins*, a book that has
meant so much to many people—including me.

THIS IS A BORZOI BOOK PUBLISHED BY ALFRED A. KNOPF

Copyright © 2001 by Sally Warner
Text illustrations copyright © 2001 by Sally Warner
Jacket illustration copyright © 2001 by George Peters

www.randomhouse.com/kids

Library of Congress Cataloging-in-Publication Data
Warner, Sally.
How to be a real person (in just one day) / by Sally Warner.
p.   cm.
Summary: Sixth grader Kara tries to conceal from her friends, her absent father,
and the authorities that her mother is sliding deeper and deeper into mental illness.
ISBN 0-375-80434-X (trade) — ISBN 0-375-90434-4 (lib. bdg.)
[1. Mentally ill—Fiction. 2. Mothers and daughters—Fiction.] I. Title.
PZ7.W24644 Ho 2001
[Fic]—dc21   00-059925

Printed in the United States of America
February 2001
10 9 8 7 6 5 4 3 2 1
First Edition

Contents

Chapter One

Thursday Morning

When I was ten years old, everything was just right—for a while. I mean it, things were almost perfect. My mom can be so much fun! She planned an Easter party that year for all our neighbors, for example. Stephanie didn't live here then, so she doesn't remember. Anyway, it was going to be the best party anyone on our street ever gave.

Me and my mom planted all these pony-packs of flowers in our garden, so it looked really nice. We got a gigantic honey-baked ham and made about a hundred little cream biscuits, and we mixed up gallons of pink punch, and we baked and decorated two cakes shaped like sitting-up rabbits, one with chocolate frosting and the other with coconut frosting. And we dyed a <u>lot</u> of Easter eggs for the big egg hunt.

My dad got into the act, too. He kept bringing things home for the party—fancy paper napkins, plastic eggs to hide goodies in, and, the day before the party, an armload of shiny Mylar rabbit balloons, enough for each kid on the street to have one.

But best of all was the piñata. Mom, Dad, and I spent a whole weekend making it. Mom planned the whole design—she's so creative sometimes! We were hoping it would look like Bugs Bunny, and we came pretty close—except we were laughing so hard when it was time to paint it that we kind of messed up. It still looked good, though.

We stuffed the piñata with candy—yellow Peeps, jelly beans, and a few chocolate bunnies—and a whole bunch of little plastic toys we got at Pic-N-Save. Each kid was going to get a turn swinging at the piñata, blindfolded, while my dad raised and lowered it by a rope looped over a branch of the Chinese elm in the backyard.

And then it rained.

But, oh no, Mom wouldn't let a little rain ruin her giant plans. She just moved the party inside, never mind the crowd or the mess. Biscuit crumbs everywhere, and jelly beans mashed into the rug? No problem.

First, we had the Easter egg hunt. We hid the eggs under sofa cushions, behind chairs, even under the beds. No place was off-limits. We were finding stinky leftover eggs for _weeks_, but Mom didn't mind.

Next came the food. My dad said he never saw a ham disappear that fast in his life. He said it was like watching a nature show about piranhas in the Amazon.

Last of all was the piñata. The littlest kids were so

excited by that time that one girl—Lulu, who lived on the corner—started crying, but we all calmed her down. My dad stood on a stepladder in the middle of the living room and held up our crazy-looking Bugs Bunny piñata, and the kids, biggest to smallest, took turns swinging an orange plastic baseball bat. One of the big kids cracked a lamp, and even <u>that</u> didn't bother my mom.

The older kids swung the hardest, but Dad let Lulu break the piñata. She was the youngest kid there. Breaking the piñata is not always such a great honor, because by the time you get your blindfold off, the treats have usually all been grabbed. Mom thought of everything, though. She had made a big treat bag for the piñata breaker, and she'd bought a little stuffed animal—a fuzzy yellow duckling—as a special prize.

Lulu cried again, but this time it was because she was so happy. I almost cried, too.

Everyone said it was the best party ever. It was pouring outside, the rain streaming down the windows as if there were some joker crouched on the roof with a hose. But inside it was spring. Balloons everywhere! And when the last neighbor left, my dad and mom and I gave each other the biggest family hug you ever saw.

Family hug, family hug, family hug.

Just like real people.

HOW TO GET READY FOR SCHOOL

1. **Get out of bed the very second the alarm goes off.** No ifs, ands, or buts! Because if you don't get up right away, you might decide never to get out of bed again. Period.

2. **Make that bed while it is still warm,** no matter how much you want to crawl back under the covers. Don't be like your mom. Pull those covers so smooth that you could never tell that a person has been sleeping there. Make it look like a department store bed.

3. **Wash your sorry, bumpy face until it shines when it's dry,** and squeegee some deodorant onto your pits so no one at school will look at you and say, "Eww, who reeks?"

4. **Get dressed in clothes that match for a change,** slob, so Marta Heinz can't make fun of you again.

5. **But remember not to call yourself names in front of any grownups at school,** or else Mr. Benito will start talking to that other teacher about your so-called self-esteem like he did last month. And self-esteem is so bogus, because why *should* everybody feel good about themselves all the time? Any kid knows the truth about this, no matter what grownups say.

6. **Tiptoe downstairs and eat a bowl of cereal, then eat another one.** Watch the little kitchen TV with the sound off so your mom doesn't wake up. Practice looking concerned, then happy, then interested in what the other guy is saying, just like the TV people. Then wash your bowl and spoon and put them away.

7. **Creep upstairs again and brush your mossy, not-perfect teeth.** Remember to use mouthwash this time, so no one at school can look at your mouth and say, "Eww, what died in there?" like Marta did that time. Leave your toothbrush sopping wet in case your mother checks it later on. Which she will, when she finally gets up. That's one thing that still makes her feel like a mom, I guess.

8. **Say good-bye nicely to your mother,** even though her bedroom door is shut.

9. **Get your backpack,** which, of course, is all ready from when you packed it last night. And try to remember all your homework for once.

10. **Go outside and take a deep, deep breath of fresh Pasadena air.** (Ha, ha.) Lock the door behind you so that no home-invasion robbers can break in and hurt your mother while you are at school.

That's the way I do it—lately, anyway, ever since Christmas vacation. And if you do everything perfectly, you feel more real.

See, that's the problem—I *don't* feel real. I don't know if I ever did. When I was a baby? Maybe. I can't remember back that far. Probably not, though. It's like there's only room for one real person in our family, and that's my mom. She wears that crown.

My mom takes up all the room, in a way, and it's as if she also breathes up all the air. Anything I do reminds her of something more interesting *she* used to do when she was a kid. Anything I try to say reminds her of something she wanted to tell me. And then she tells me—and *tells* me.

Anything I feel, she feels more.

It's like this joke I heard once. Well, I didn't get the actual joke, but I sure understood the punch line: "When I die, her life will flash before my eyes."

Not my own life, *her* life.

That's exactly right! For example, I can't remember when I lost my first tooth, but I can tell you every detail about when my mom lost hers. I don't know how I got the little scar on my ankle, but I know all about the time my mom's finger got mashed between two benches when she was in the second grade. I can't remember my first day of kindergarten, much less what I was wearing, but Mom was *terrified* on her first day, even though she had on a beautiful new blue dress.

6

Stuff like that, only multiplied by a thousand. And it's always been this way.

Can I talk to my father about this? No. I'm pretty sure he doesn't feel real, either. That might be the reason he left.

Can I talk to my mother about this? Dumb me—I actually tried once, when she was in one of her really good moods. She said, "Oh, Kara, of course you're real! I gave birth to you, didn't I?" And then she told me *that* long, icky story all over again.

I'm real because she had me. Like that's supposed to be enough.

Weird things make me feel a little bit real, such as doing the same things in the same way each day—as perfectly as I can.

Chewing my fingernails down until my fingertips hurt makes me feel a little bit real.

Repeating two or three words in my head over and over does, too.

Or thinking about Lonely Island. I'm the only person living there, so I *must* be real.

The elephant seals think I'm real as I watch them loll on the beach like living boulders; the crafty, begging gulls think I'm real as they haunt my campsite for scraps of food; the sun thinks I'm real as it warms my shoulders like a cormorant feather cloak; the salty wind thinks I'm real as it blows around me, so strong sometimes that I almost fall over.

"Island, island," I whisper after rinsing out my mouth for the last time. I grin at myself in the bathroom mirror. There I stand, flip-flopped in the mirror's shiny surface: straight blond hair, round blue eyes.

Cheerful-looking round white face.

A few freckles.

Navy-and-white-striped long-sleeved T-shirt, as baggy as I can buy without my mom sitting me down for the what-a-nice-figure-you-have talk. Khaki pants.

I leave my toothbrush lying at the edge of the sink in a little puddle of water—but like I said earlier, I do it on purpose.

I step into the upstairs hall. "Good-bye, Mom," I call out softly, my mouth minty-fresh. Uh-oh, there are a couple of foamy toothpaste speckles on my shirt. I scritch at them with a gnawed-down fingernail.

My mom's bedroom door is all scraped at the bottom where Feather used to scratch, trying to get in. That was when she *wanted* to get in the room—when my dad was still living here. Next to me, Feather liked my dad best. Mom wasn't on Feather's list.

That was before my mom took Feather to the animal shelter. Mom was still driving then.

I don't want to think about losing Feather, but I can't help it. I think about it *hard* as I wedge my homework into

8

the old dark red backpack that is sitting at the end of my neatly made bed. Fitting everything inside that bag each night is like doing a really complicated Chinese puzzle, only big—but I have saved room for my homework. "Feather, Feather, Feather," I say softly.

My mom says that even the most innocent animals can carry disease. They might also turn and attack their owners—she's read all about it. She says that Feather went to a happy home.

What a liar.

I had a dream the first night my dog was gone. She was floating up, up, up in the midnight air like—like a Feather balloon. And then she just floated away.

I think she's dead—just like Rontu in the book.

Rontu, my island companion.

Okay.

My mother is still asleep as I tiptoe down the stairs. That's not so unusual! Lots of grownups sleep in. She stays up late worrying, she says.

I guess that's supposed to make me feel bad.

I don't know what she does alone in her room all night other than worry, but even when I get up at two A.M., like if I have a nightmare and want to go down the hall to the bathroom and get a drink of water, I can see a skinny strip of light glowing under her door. And it's not blue TV light, either.

She's just awake, that's all. Awake and smoking. The

9

stink floats out from under the door. And she's drinking, probably—*clink, clink.* Sometimes I even hear her arguing—with herself, I guess. Or maybe she's making prank phone calls. Who knows?

But I'm not supposed to bother her, so I can't ask what's wrong.

I make sure the kitchen is tidy before slipping out the back door. Black-and-white vinyl squares on the floor, a drippy sink, and a dishwasher that hasn't worked for the last six weeks. But the counters are spotless, the faded old dish towel with roosters on it is folded into thirds just the way my mom likes, and the refrigerator is droning away— like some absent-minded chatterbox you can only escape by leaving the room.

Our house is kind of old for a California house—it was built in 1920. We live on a nice street where the branches of the camphor trees planted along each side bend and tangle to make a shady tunnel down the middle of the road. Our house is near the end of the block. It is two stories high. It has four bedrooms and two and a half bathrooms, whatever half a bathroom is. The half bathroom has a toilet, anyway, and that's the important part.

My mom has her own bathroom. It used to be my dad's, too, until he left three days after Christmas because of his new job up in Santa Barbara. But by then, I don't think my mom even liked having him in the house, so that was okay. My mom wouldn't move to Santa Barbara, so now my dad sends us money.

He doesn't know anything's wrong. Anything new, that is—and I'm afraid to tell him, because what would he say?

Move to Santa Barbara? Yeah, but what would happen to my mom?

I'll come back to Pasadena right away? Yeah, but then what? He'd lose his Santa Barbara job, and we'd be poor. He and my mom would just start yelling at each other again, and that would make things even worse.

Or would he say, *You can't manage this all by yourself!?*

Oh, yes I can. I'm doing it, aren't I?

My dad's been gone for two months. It's true that my mom has practically lived in her bedroom for the last eight weeks, which I guess, among other things, means she can't stand the sight of me. But things will get better—if I can just keep other people from finding out about us. Things are under control.

Sometimes, though, I feel like one of those ghosts on a TV show—you know, the way they can shimmer and then start to disappear right before your very eyes? Whenever they want to?

I don't know why this is. I don't want to disappear, though. I guess I'm trying to do the opposite. I'm trying to be real.

My mom gets mad whenever she even hears the words

Santa Barbara. She says it's just red tiles and palm trees up there, red tiles and palm trees. But she gets that way about stuff sometimes. I have to admit it's gotten worse since Christmas, no matter how much I try to take care of her.

Nowadays, for my mom a bad thought is like a splinter that gets into the palm of your hand. She wiggles it and wiggles it, trying to get that splinter out, and it only hurts a little. But all of a sudden it hurts a whole lot—because by then it's infected.

I like Santa Barbara, though. I've visited my dad up there—only once so far, because my mother won't drive anymore. My dad came down to get me on Valentine's Day weekend. Mom said that I couldn't run out to his car, either—she made him ring the doorbell like a stranger.

When he walked up the path, he looked like he was on his way to the dentist to get all his teeth drilled or something.

It can take two hours to get up to Santa Barbara from Pasadena, and two hours to get back—not even in rush hour! and that's if your old gray Honda Accord doesn't break down!—so my dad was driving for practically the whole weekend. Down and up, down and up. I could tell it was hard to take that much time away from his new job, even though it was the weekend. He works hard.

We had fun, though. We walked along State Street and ate ice cream cones next to a pretty tiled fountain in a shopping arcade. We walked around the harbor and watched a big boat named *Truth* get ready to leave on a half-day fishing trip. We saw some students from the university learning to sail. We didn't talk about my mother.

Well, he didn't ask, and I didn't want to ruin our time together. He said he was sorry six weeks had gone by already, but it had taken him a while to get settled.

That was two weeks ago.

My mother is right about the red tiles and palm trees up in Santa Barbara. The whole town is covered with them! There's probably a law about it.

I say good-bye to the kitchen and leave for school. I always lock the door behind me. See, that's another important thing. Because like I started to say before, ever since my dad left, my mom is even more afraid than usual about home-invasion robberies. She reads about them in the newspaper.

Her eyes are like magnets when she reads the paper. They go straight to the weirdest disaster stories you've ever read, no matter how small the article is. *Man saws off arm while carving Christmas turkey! Woman drowns while brushing her teeth! Killer bees are heading your way!*

Also, she never misses stories about carjackings—which she says is why she gave up driving. But that's okay, because there's no place that we really have to go.

Especially not Santa Barbara.

● ● ●

"Hi, Kara," Stephanie calls out. Her house is in the middle of our block, and she waits for me out front most mornings so we can walk to school together. "How's your mom?" She asks me that a lot.

Stephanie Miller's family moved in after Christmas, just about the time my dad left.

"She's feeling a little bit better," I lie. It's a lie because my mother isn't really sick. She does not have a fever. Even if she catches the flu or something, she won't go to the doctor anymore. She says that doctors are just in it for the money. She says she wouldn't trust a doctor farther than she could throw him.

But my-mother-being-sick is just something all the neighbors started telling themselves, I guess, to explain everything. Like why she didn't move to Santa Barbara with my dad.

Like why we get groceries delivered to our house instead of shopping for them like normal people.

Like about my Feather balloon floating away.

Like why I never invite other kids over—not that I ever did, much.

See, that's why Stephanie and I are such good friends. She never knew my family could be any other way than the way it is now. To Stephanie, I am exactly like a real person.

14

But also, I like Stephanie because she is nice—and funny, too. This is a surprise, because she has such a serious face. Her forehead is always a little bit wrinkled, as if she has only now remembered that she forgot to study for a big math test. Then she says something that is the last thing that you would expect a worried-looking person like her to say, and you just have to start laughing.

Like that time she told me that our teacher, Mr. Benito, reminded her of Grover on *Sesame Street*! I can't explain it, but she's exactly right—they have the same burbly voice, for one thing. We've called him Grover ever since, when we are alone.

She thinks I'm funny, too.

Stephanie and I look like exact opposites. She has curly black hair that goes way out, and brown eyes the color of acorns. She is short and skinny. I have straight blond hair and blue eyes, and I'm tall and not-skinny.

In other words, fat. Or almost-fat. Not circus-lady fat, though.

It's strange that Stephanie is the one who looks like she just got put in charge of the global warming thing and I'm the one with the pale, moonlike face that has a care-free expression on it. Because really, like I said before, it's just the opposite!

Anyway, we're in the same sixth-grade class together at Maybeck Middle School.

"Did you bring your book report?" Stephanie asks me.

"Remember, Grover said you had to do your oral presentation today, no excuses."

"I've got it," I say, shifting my backpack as if the report just gave a little bounce in there. I don't tell Stephanie that I have no *intention* of doing an oral presentation, though. No way am I going to stand up in front of everyone. They'd probably be able to see right through me. "You're lucky you already did yours," I say.

"I liked my book," she points out, as if making an excuse for herself.

"Well, I liked mine, too," I say. "I just don't like standing there in front of everyone and his dog to tell why. It's *private*."

"Grover says that public speaking is an important skill for any young man or lady to learn," she says, doing a perfect imitation of him. I can practically see the shaggy blue fur!

I snort. "Yeah, if you're planning a career as a blabbermouth," I say.

Stephanie laughs. "Melena wants to be a lawyer. Does that count?" she asks, naming this other girl in our class. Her real name is Marie Elena Vasquez, but it's Melena for short.

"Definitely," I say. "But she'll be a *nice* blabbermouth." Melena is okay, I guess.

Sometimes Stephanie weaves narrow strands of her springy black hair into one long, skinny braid with beads in it. She did today, and the braid falls against her cheek.

She could be Tutok.

Tutok, Aleut girl. My only human friend—until she left the island.

Okay.

"What do you want to be when you grow up?" she asks me, tugging at the end of her Tutok braid.

Usually I give her a joke-answer when she asks me something serious like that. "A hermit," I say now.

Which is only *kind of* a joke-answer.

The real answer is—I don't know what I want to be when I grow up! Only whatever it is, I'll be living alone. Alone is when you feel the most real.

"A hermit *crab?*" Stephanie asks, teasing.

"If necessary," I tell her.

I am not smiling when I say this.

Chapter Two

Still Thursday

It was the Monday after last Fourth of July, and my dad had just gotten home from work—with a surprise for me. "A puppy! Oh my gosh, oh my gosh," I said, gathering up the squirmy little animal into my arms. She was pure white, just like a marshmallow ice cream sundae, and her long tail curled around my arm. "Oh, thank you, Daddy— I always wanted a dog." I sniffed the dog's hot, furry neck, and it smelled good, like lemons.

I could see Mom's foot tapping, though, and she let out a mouthful of smoke with a loud whoosh. "Big hero," she said, shooting an angry look at my dad, and she smashed out her cigarette in a houseplant. A plant that my dad had brought home just the week before. "Bi-i-ig hero," she repeated, dragging out the word. "Don't expect me to take care of it. As if I didn't have enough to do already," she added, giving me a dirty look. I held still, as if we were playing Statues and she had just whirled around.

She lit another cigarette. It was bent in the middle.

"I couldn't resist," my dad told her. "Kara will take care of her," he said, please-please-please in his voice.

I hated hearing that please-please-please, but I didn't blame my dad. Not really. My mom can be kind of scary sometimes, she gets so mad. She thinks people are laughing at her. Even when she's not mad, she's <u>almost</u> mad. She's like a pot of bean-with-bacon soup that's just about to boil. Or else—just like that!—she turns into the happiest person in the world. And that can be scary, too, believe it or not.

But every so often, she slows down so much that she won't even get out of bed. Things are better then, to tell the truth—or they were when my dad was still living with us.

Mom pointed at the puppy. "You did this just to hurt me, didn't you?" she said to my dad. "You can't resist that, either."

Nobody but me was paying any attention at all to the puppy, whose long, plume-y tail was starting to droop because of the angry voices. She wet a little on my shirt. I started to edge toward the door.

"Take a chill pill, hon," my dad said, trying to sound casual. "Or take some kind of pill," he muttered.

"Oh, that's your answer to everything, isn't it?" Mom cried. "You and that doctor of mine! You're probably in this together, and I told you both I don't like stuffing my body with chemicals. And don't call me hon, <u>hon</u>."

"You know you have to take your pills, Margery," my dad said. I thought that took guts.

The puppy and I were almost at the door.

"I don't _have_ to do anything," my mom snapped.

Escape.

In the hall, the puppy's tail gave a tiny practice wag, as if it were asking a question. "Feather," I said, deciding on her name.

I combed her silky fur with cold fingers.

HOW TO GET OUT OF GIVING AN ORAL PRESENTATION

1. **Stay home from school.**
2. **If that doesn't work, go to school**—but "forget" to bring your report.
3. **If _that_ doesn't work, get sent to the school nurse if she's there that day**—but only pretend to be a little sick or else they'll call your mother. And that would be a disaster.
4. **If _that_ doesn't work, say that you have to go to the bathroom just before Mr. Benito calls your name.** And then stay there.
5. **If _that_ doesn't work, tell Mr. Benito that you already gave your oral presentation, doesn't he remember?**

"I gave it on Tuesday, don't you remember? About an Indian girl who lived alone on an island? A Native American girl, I mean," I correct myself. I did not plan to mention my book out loud to the class, but I panicked.

Next to me, Howard Matthews yawns big-time and starts fiddling with his hair again. He wants dreadlocks, but he has floppy blond skateboard-kid hair, so good luck.

I sneak a peek at Stephanie.

Mr. Benito runs his finger along a line in his notebook, frowning. "No-o-o," he says slowly. "In fact," he adds, flipping back a page, "according to my records, you haven't given one oral presentation since the week after Thanksgiving."

And it's almost March, too! I've just about pulled it off. "Are you sure you're on the right line?" I ask him. "It's Kara Biggs. B-I-G-G-S."

"I know how to spell your name, Kara," Mr. Benito says, scowling a little.

"I'm sorry," I say, pretending.

"Well, I'm sorry, too," Mr. Benito says, "but you're going to have to give your report again."

"*Again?* But—but I don't know if I brought it today," I tell him. "It's in my other notebook, I think. The one that I left at home."

"Then do it from memory," he says.

Mr. Benito is looking less like Grover and more like Oscar the Grouch every second.

Kids are shifting in their seats the way they do just before someone gets in big trouble. Even Howard Matthews is waking up a little. It's like in nature, when sharks smell blood in the water. I read a library book about that once.

Stephanie raises her hand. "I'll give *my* presentation again, Mr. Benito," she says. "A couple of kids missed it. And I think Kara has a fever."

I lift my hand to my forehead, and a worried expression settles on my face. I try to look hot. "Maybe I should go to the nurse," I say, my voice faint.

Mr. Benito walks over to me and touches my forehead with one finger, like E.T. "Maybe I should call your parents," Mr. Benito says.

My parents! He *can't* call my house, because of course my mother would be the one to answer the phone, and who knows what she'd say to him? "No, that's okay," I say, springing to my feet. "I think I can do it."

Only now I can't give my book report using notes like everyone else, because I told Mr. Benito—*Grover*—that I left everything in my other notebook. The one that's supposedly at home. And I don't even have another notebook.

Luckily, I know this book by heart. It is called *Island of the Blue Dolphins*, and it is not only my favorite book, it has saved my life, practically. I discovered it all by myself, too—well, with the help of Mrs. Foley, who works in the kids' room at the big library on Walnut Street. She

22

doesn't just know baby books and those prom books they always throw at girls my age, she also knows good ones.

The point is, I didn't need Mr. Benito to tell me to read it. I don't see why books have to be like this punishment or something.

I take the long, long walk to the front of the room, and I turn to face the class. And I think: My clothes match. My face is clean. I used deodorant. And mouthwash.

I can hear the surf pounding in my ears. The waves are like my own heartbeat.

Howard Matthews is looking at me with half-crossed eyes, but he always does that. There is no reason for anyone in class to think that there is anything wrong with me.

There *isn't*.

I drag myself away from Lonely Island and back to the classroom. "Okay," I begin. My voice is a little hoarse. "The book I read is—"

"Introduce yourself and give us the name of the book and the author," Mr. Benito interrupts.

"Okay," I say again, even though introducing yourself is the most bogus part about giving an oral presentation. I mean, it's the end of February. If the kids in my class don't know each others' names by now, what hope is there?

But I clear my throat. "My name is Kara Biggs, and the book I read is called *Island of the Blue Dolphins*. It's by Mr. Scott O'Dell."

"You can just say 'Scott O'Dell,' Kara," Mr. Benito interrupts again.

I turn to him. "But my mother and father told me always to say Mr. or Mrs. for a grownup," I tell him. I try to peek at the clock without Mr. Benito seeing me. Maybe if I can dawdle long enough, it will be time for midmorning break.

But *no*. "Continue, please," Mr. Benito says.

"Well, the book is called *Island of the Blue Dolphins*, and it's by—by Scott O'Dell." I clear my throat again. I look over at Stephanie, hoping that will give me strength.

She crosses her fingers and raises them just high enough over the top of her desk for me to see them.

"Continue," Mr. Benito says again.

"Okay. Well, it's mostly a true story. It's about this girl who lives with her tribe—it's a very *small* tribe—on an island they call 'Island of the Blue Dolphins.' It's a real place, sort of near Catalina Island."

I pause, and sure enough, a couple of kids start to whisper, because they have been to Catalina. I have heard them bragging about it during the year, especially Marta Heinz. But she brags about everything. She would probably brag about what she had for breakfast. "I ate the most amazing pancake!" Sure enough, her hand shoots up into the air.

"Yes, Marta?" Mr. Benito asks.

Marta wriggles in her seat, looking important. Her

24

square face is flushed even pinker than usual. "Well, but it can't be a true story," she says, "because there *is* no such island. I know all the Channel Islands, and that's not one of them."

"We call the island San Nicolas now," Mr. Benito says, surprising me. "It's the farthest out. The military uses it. Continue," he repeats.

"Okay," I say. "Well, this boat comes to take her tribe away from the island, and it's hard to explain, but they don't mind going. Only, when she's on the boat, the girl sees that her little brother got left behind. She can't make the boat go back for him, because there's a storm coming, so she jumps overboard and swims back to the island. And then they're stranded."

Howard is excited for once. His hand goes up. "Why doesn't someone just get a helicopter to go rescue them?" he asks before Mr. Benito has even called on him.

"Perhaps Kara can answer that question for us," Mr. Benito says. "Kara?"

I clear my throat. "It's because this whole thing happened way in the past. More than a hundred years ago. They didn't have helicopters then," I tell Howard—who has already lost interest. He just wanted to say something, it didn't matter what.

"More like a hundred and fifty years ago," Mr. Benito chimes in, surprising me again. He really knows this story!

Marta has slumped back into her seat. It is as if she is

saying, *Who <u>cares</u> what happened a hundred and fifty years ago?*
She examines the chipped blue polish on her fingernails
and then nibbles a little on one finger as if it is a potato chip
that has just been dipped into something yummy.

Wearing nail polish. That's something real I could do.

"Continue," Mr. Benito says.

But I don't *want* to continue! I have been trapped
into giving an oral presentation about a book that means
something private to me. And all Howard Matthews
wants is for some rescue squad to come swooping in with
helicopters and submarines, probably, and all Marta
Heinz wants is to show how wrong I am about the Channel Islands. Nobody's even listening to the important
things about the story.

"Kara?" Mr. Benito prompts.

He wants me to tell about how the girl's little brother
got killed by wild dogs almost immediately. He wants the
class to hear how she tried to escape the island in a canoe,
how she tamed one of the wild dogs, how she almost got
killed by the devilfish, by a tidal wave. . . .

He wants me to say how she had to live all by herself
on that island for years and years and years, surrounded by
things that scared her. But I won't. Enough is enough.
This island is *mine.*

"Well, that's just about it," I tell him—and the class.
"It's a really good book. But to find out how it ends, you'll
just have to read it yourself!" That's the way practically

everyone finishes their oral presentations in our class. Sometimes, hearing those words is the only way you know a person's presentation is over.

This time it doesn't work. A couple of baffled-looking kids are whispering together, and one or two hands are slowly raised.

Mr. Benito ignores them, though. "Kara," he says, a very serious look on his face, "is that really all you have to tell the class about this book?"

I bite my lip and look up, as if I am thinking. "Just about," I finally say, trying to sound breezy. "It's pretty much an adventure story! With a lot of nature in it."

My teacher has been sitting perched on the edge of his desk. Now he stands up tall and smooths his hair back with both hands, as if what I just said is the last straw. "Did you even *read* the book?" he asks quietly.

Chapter

More Thursday

Last May, my mom was in one of her happy moods—scary-happy, not fun-happy—and she went out shopping and spent a lot of money. A <u>lot</u> of money. She bought new clothes for my dad, for me, and for herself—especially for herself. She said, "I'm tired of going around in rags. I deserve better than this."

I have to admit that I loved some of the clothes she bought me. Well, who doesn't like new clothes? Except I wanted to choose my own stuff. I was almost twelve then. I wasn't a baby anymore! And she bought me four bathing suits, when between you and me I really just needed two for the summer, and six pairs of shorts, and seven T-shirts. And a few dresses, too, in show-offy colors that I would never choose for myself.

It was like she wanted me to be someone else—the bright, perky person she wished <u>she</u> was, maybe.

My mom was actually surprised when my dad got

mad at her. "But you need new khakis," she pointed out.

"Yeah, but Ralph Laurens? And four pairs?" my dad almost groaned. "Who's going to pay for this stuff, Marge?"

"Oh, you're such a bore," my mom said, throwing up her hands. "You ought to be thanking me! You're <u>welcome</u>," she said, all sarcastic.

My dad shook his head. "You promised you wouldn't do this again, hon, not after the last time. You said you would leave the credit cards at home. We just finished paying off—"

"I'm not going to walk around Pasadena without a credit card in my handbag," she interrupted. She said "walk," only she hadn't been walking, she'd been driving. And she'd gotten two speeding tickets in one week—but my dad didn't know about those yet. "Anyway," my mom continued, "half these things were on sale. I saved you a ton of money. And stop calling me <u>hon</u>."

"Of course I read the book," I tell Mr. Benito in a shaky voice. I can feel my face turn red. I don't think that Mr. Benito has ever asked a kid this question before, no matter how stupid they just sounded. I peek around, wishing that I could just run out the door and never come back. Poor Stephanie is sinking down behind her desk as if she is melting. And Marta is perking up. So is Howard.

Send a helicopter to rescue *me*, Howard!

Dial 911!

"All right, then," Mr. Benito says, his voice soft—soft and hard at the same time. "What was the girl's secret name?"

The girl's secret name.

30

Okay. I happen to know the answer to this question very well, but I'm not going to say her name out loud. I learned that much from the book. If you say a secret name out loud, it loses its power—and *anything* could happen.

What if all of a sudden I couldn't get to Lonely Island anymore—then where would I be? Lost.

The entire class is waiting. Even the *clock* is waiting. The minute hand hasn't moved in ages—and I know, because I've been watching it. "Her brother's name was Ramo," I finally say, as if I am on a TV game show and I am trying to prove that I know at least *part* of the answer.

"I've read that book," Stephanie chimes in, trying to help me out. "He's the one who got eaten by the wild dogs."

"Raise your hand next time, Stephanie," Mr. Benito tells her.

"The wild dogs didn't *eat* Ramo," I say to the class. "They just killed him."

Suddenly, it's as if the minute hand on the classroom clock just remembered it is supposed to be keeping time, and it jumps ahead a couple of minutes with a loud *click*. The bell goes off for midmorning break.

"Excused," Mr. Benito calls out. "All except for you, Ms. Biggs. I'd like you to stay."

"But—but I can't," I whisper. "I need to go to the bathroom." Which is a lie, but *he* doesn't know that.

"This will just take a minute of your time," he tells me. He sits down behind his desk. I stand in front of him as kids jump from their seats and start pawing through their backpacks like—well, like a pack of wild dogs looking for something to eat.

Uh-oh. Nothing good happens when someone says, *This will just take a minute of your time.* Ever.

We wait for the last nosy stragglers to leave the room. "Mr. Benito, I *did* read the book," I say as the door finally closes.

"This isn't only about the book," Mr. Benito says. "Your work in general has been slipping lately, Kara. You leave assignments at home, you don't do your share of the work on group projects. I think we need to have a family conference."

A family conference!

What family?

I don't say that, though. "It's just hard for me to get to the library after school," I tell him. I leave out the part about how my mother says she'll call the police if I'm not home twenty minutes after my last class is out. She'd do it, too!

And then what would happen? *She'd* probably be the one to get hauled away.

My poor mom.

A concerned look sweeps across Mr. Benito's face. "Kara," he says, "is there a problem going on in your life? Something I should know about?"

Hmm, I think sarcastically—that's a tough one. Something he should know about? But why? So he could start taking care of me and my mom? Order the groceries? Make her dinner? Pay the bills?

I don't *think* so.

My dad is trying to help. He wants me to come live with him in Santa Barbara, he says, but he has to handle things just right so my mom doesn't freak about it. These things take time, he says. He thinks everything is okay at home. Well, not okay exactly, but the same as usual.

At first, my dad called me every night—or he tried to call. My mom would grab for the phone, though, and then either slam it down when she heard his voice or start yelling at him about money and stuff.

So my dad started calling me every *other* night, then twice a week.

Now he tries to call once a week, but it's a miracle if I can talk to him without my mom listening in.

Supposedly, I can call him collect whenever I want, but he's hardly ever home. He eats most of his meals at this coffee shop on Milpas Street.

I have my dad's work number, but the office manager usually answers, and I get shy and don't know what to say. "Is this an emergency?" she asks.

"I guess not," I say.

"Is there a problem at home, Kara?" Mr. Benito says again.

"I guess not," I say.

No, if I told Mr. Benito that there was a problem, he would just fill out some form or something—do the paperwork. Get it off his chest. And *I'd* be the one stuck with the results. People prying around our house—or who knows what. Huge trouble for my mom, though, and she doesn't need any more trouble, believe me.

If some stranger came to the door asking questions, she'd probably *completely* flip.

No, it's up to me to hold everything together, which is what I am doing. I just need people to mind their own business long enough for things to get back to normal, that's all. I know my mom will get better if she can just have some peace and quiet.

"I can't think of any problems," I say in my most thoughtful voice. "Everything in my life is just about perfect. I guess I'm just not a very good student, that's all. Not everyone can be a brain."

Mr. Benito thinks for a moment. He is still looking concerned. "Well, I don't know about that," he finally says, "but maybe a family conference will help clear things up." He rises from his chair, like that's that.

"But we *can't* have a family conference. Not for a couple more weeks," I say, trying to stall him—and struggling to keep my voice normal. "My parents are away on business. There's just a housekeeper at home, and she doesn't speak English very well."

"Business, eh?" Mr. Benito asks. "I think that's what you told me a month ago, Kara. Your parents must do an awful lot of business traveling."

"Well, it's more like a funeral, really," I say, inventing a new story on the spot. "It's a combination business trip and funeral—because my grandmother, she died." I try to look sad and, to my surprise, tears fill my eyes. "My mother and father didn't want me to miss any school or I would have gone to the funeral, too," I tell him, sniffling a little.

"Hmm," Mr. Benito says. "Well, I think I'll just call your house anyway and talk with the housekeeper. Find out when your parents will be back."

"But I told you, she—"

"I know," he interrupts. "She doesn't speak much English. Don't worry, I'll manage."

"Mr. Benito, you just *can't* call my house!"

"Why, Kara? Is the phone broken again?" he asks me, but not in a mean way.

I forgot I'd used that one on him already. "N-n-n-no," I say, speaking slowly but trying to think fast. "It's just . . . It's kind of personal, I guess."

A satisfied now-we're-getting-someplace look spreads across Mr. Benito's face. "What's the problem, Kara?" he asks, his voice soft.

The tears spill down my cheeks.

I hate him.

"It's my aunt," I blurt out, wiping my cheeks with the back of my hand. I may be crying, but I can still lie. "She's staying with us for a while. And—well, I'm sorry to say this, but she's kind of..." I can't think of what my pretend aunt is *kind of*, so my voice fades.

"Kind of?" Mr. Benito asks gently, his brown eyes urging me to continue.

"Well, she'll probably grab for the phone, and she's kind of nutty, that's all. She's taking medicine for it," I add, trying to reassure him, "but she'd be really upset to hear a strange man's voice. So *please* don't call! Give me a note and I'll take it home to my mother. And my father. They'll call you back and make an appointment."

Mr. Benito stares at me for a moment, then hands me a Kleenex and sighs. "All right," he says, ripping a piece of notebook paper from his binder and starting to write. "But I'm going to be following up, Kara. This is an important school year for you, and you're too smart to simply throw it all away."

There is nothing simple about this, I want to tell him. "Thank you," I say, taking the note. I ignore his so-called compliment, though, because he doesn't really think I'm smart at all. He has brainy pets, like Marta, Melena, and even Stephanie. But I'm definitely not one of them.

I'm not too worried about him following up on the note, by the way. He always says he's going to, but he usually forgets stuff like that because he's so busy.

Anyway, I'll figure out what to do about that when it happens.

"I've had to give you a D on your oral presentation, Kara," Mr. Benito is saying. "That means 'noticeably weak,' by the way. I'll take your word for it that you actually read the book, but your report *was* noticeably weak. I'm sure you'll do better next time."

"Okay," I say, and I fold his note into tiny squares and jam it into my pocket.

"Break's almost over, I'm afraid," Mr. Benito says, "but you still have time to use the rest room. I'm going to go check my messages." He leaves the room.

And I can't resist it. I fish a piece of scrap paper out of the wastebasket, tear off a corner, find a pencil, and write down the word *Karana*.

Which is the girl's secret name—the one in my book.

I put the scrap of paper on the edge of his desk, where Mr. Benito will be sure to see it. I want him to know that I know.

Not that it's usually such a bad thing when people think you're noticeably weak. It keeps them off your back.

I'll just have to try for a C next time.

Chapter Four

Thursday Lunch

Before Christmas, I sometimes felt that watching my mom live her life was a little like watching a surfer. My dad and I used to go to the beach a lot, so I've had practice doing that.

In Southern California, surfers cram themselves into wet suits that let them go in the water even in winter, and stay out there for hours on end. They paddle out past the breaking waves, then straddle their boards, turn their backs to the shore, and gaze out to sea, waiting for the perfect ride. They rise with the swells, then dip into the troughs between the waves, watching and waiting.

They only catch a wave and ride it to shore every so often—and even then, they usually don't come in all the way. Instead, toward the end of their ride, they walk the nose of the board backward over the lip of the wave and head back out to sea without ever jumping off.

Now, understand, my mom has never gone surfing in

her life. I know that for a fact, because she would have talked about it a lot, believe me. But I still say she is <u>like</u> a surfer.

Watching her, it was as though my imaginary surfer-mom would slowly go up, up, up with a swell that could last one month, or two, or even three, and then almost disappear between the waves, the troughs might get so deep.

In real life, that meant she would race around shopping or fighting or throwing parties for a while, and then she would just crawl into bed and cry. For a long time.

And before Christmas, it was as though I was standing on the shore holding a towel for her instead of living a life of my own. I'd watch her go up, down.

Up, down.

Still, whether my mom was up or down, most of the time she wouldn't turn around to face the shore no matter how loud I yelled.

In other words, whether she was happy or sad, she didn't really seem to think much about me—or my dad, for that matter. Her changing moods were just random, like the surf. But no matter how great the wave was that she'd just caught, pretty soon she would head back out to the deep water.

In real life, that meant crashing down again and going back to bed.

I have learned these things the hard way.

Last spring, she almost made it all the way to shore—for good, I thought. (Ha, ha.) Between Christmas and Easter she was fun-happy, not scary-happy, and we were just like a real family. She was seeing her doctor every week, and she wasn't mad at anyone much. Naturally, my dad was happy too, but he was watching her—waiting for things to change—and so was I.

We would go out to dinner on Sunday nights. "Our family always goes out together on Sundays. It's so boring," I'd say at school the next morning, pretending that it was a usual thing and I hated it.

We even went down to Baja California for spring break, even though we had a lot of bills to pay. "Do you want to bring a friend?" my dad asked me—which was not a fair question, really, because who was I going to ask? I'd spent the whole school year <u>not</u> making friends, because friends expect to be invited over to your house every so often. And how in the world could I do that?

"No thanks," I said.

We had fun, the three of us—until she turned away to paddle back out to sea.

HOW TO BE UN-NOTICEABLY STRONG

1. **Don't tell other people your troubles.**
2. **If they ask, lie.**
3. **If the lie doesn't work, tell another lie, and then another.** Pretty soon people will believe you—or else they'll get so worn out that they'll stop asking questions.
4. **Whatever you do, don't start feeling sorry for yourself.**
5. **If you do feel sorry for yourself, keep your mouth shut**—because if you don't, things will only get worse. Fast.

"What was all *that* about?" Stephanie asks me in the hallway. We are in line for the drinking fountain. She is standing right behind me. I know that by the time it is my turn to drink, the water will be trickling out of the spout in a pathetic little burble—which is probably very unsanitary to drink from.

Thanks a lot, *Grover.*

"Oh, he only wanted to ask me some more questions about that book I did the report on," I tell her, fibbing easily. "I guess he figured I was just too shy to do a good job in front of the class."

"But things are okay now?" Stephanie asks, the worry lines in her forehead deepening.

"Pretty much okay," I tell her. "Go ahead," I urge when it is finally my turn. "You go first." She flips her black hair over her shoulders and holds it back with one hand.

"Hey, no fair!" a skinny kid behind us squawks. "No jumping ahead in line."

It's a weird thing about middle school boys. Some of the sixth graders still look like little kids, all short and peanut buttery, and some of the eighth graders look like grownups, all hulking and whiskery. It's the same with the girls, only without the whiskers.

This is one of the peanut butter boys.

I turn around and glare at him while Stephanie bends her head and drinks. He is all sweaty from running around outside. "What difference is it to you, stupid?" I ask. "We were both in front of you anyway." I'm usually not this mean, especially to boys, but right now it feels good.

"It's just not fair," he sort of whines, embarrassed. He looks around as if hoping that someone—anyone—will back him up. "It's against the rules," he adds. He reminds me of a teensy version of some news guy on TV, all fakey-mad about lawbreakers.

Stephanie is delicately dabbing her drippy mouth with

the pink sleeve of her turtleneck. "It's all yours," she tells me.

"I'm not thirsty anymore," I inform her—and the straggly line of kids behind us. "I'll let Mr. Rules here have my turn."

I look back at the drinking fountain as we walk to class, and I see the boy pounce greedily on the feeble spout of water. He's practically sucking on the chrome.

Yuck.

"Did you bring your lunch today?" Stephanie asks at lunchtime. I don't know why she hasn't given up on this idea by now.

"No. My mother didn't have time to pack it," I tell her for what seems like the hundredth time. "She wasn't feeling well enough, so she just sent me with lunch money."

"You should pack your lunch yourself," Stephanie says. "That way we could trade stuff."

Yeah, I think—except *what* stuff? Frozen dinners? Frozen dinners, gigantic boxes of cereal, heavy plastic jugs of milk, bottles of wine, and big sacks of oranges. That's what my mother orders from the store, mostly. She says that just about covers it.

I can see it now: "Here, Stephanie—want to trade half of your homemade tuna fish sandwich for a nice hunk of my Salisbury steak? It's almost thawed out!"

43

Right.

My mother leaves lunch money on the kitchen table. It's there as if by magic, first thing every morning— even though I don't ever hear her creeping downstairs to leave it.

And when would I have time to pack a lunch? In between washing my cereal bowl, getting clean wrinkly clothes that match from the dryer (assuming I remembered to put the wet clothes *in* the dryer the night before, that is), making my bed and all that stuff I already said, and, Mr. Benito's personal favorite, forgetting my homework?

No, I have my hands full enough already. Not that I can't manage.

"At least we get to eat together," I point out. Because at Maybeck Middle School, they let lunch-box kids eat in the cafeteria if they want, and they let cafeteria kids take their trays out onto the caged-in patio if *they* want. The patio is where Stephanie and I usually eat, if it's not raining—which it hardly ever is. Ellen Cho and Melena Vasquez eat with us, too. Melena is the one who wants to be a lawyer. They're in the other sixth-grade class, those luckies. "Save me a seat," I tell Stephanie.

I let Melena get in front of me in line so I can watch her. She usually buys her lunch, too. I get what she gets. Today she chooses a burrito, fruit cup, and lemonade. I chew on my lip and pretend that I am making up my

44

mind. A grilled cheese sandwich? Chocolate pudding? Milk?

Hmm. No, a burrito, fruit cup, and lemonade looks good to me.

"Grover was really picking on Kara this morning. It was so harsh," Stephanie tells the others as Melena and I sit down under a towering eucalyptus tree. Stephanie pulls plastic containers out of her lunch box as she says this. The sixth graders at my school still bring lunch boxes to school, the more colorful the better. Sometimes I bring one, too, with big Sixties daisies on it, only I keep pencils and stuff inside.

"It was no big deal," I say. I watch Stephanie and Ellen unpack their lunch boxes. I keep track of what they bring, in case I ever start packing my own lunch. That's how you learn.

The main thing is, their food is different colors. They wouldn't bring a sandwich on white bread, potato chips, and macaroni salad, for example, because those things are all the same color. But they might bring a sandwich, celery sticks, an apple, and a brownie.

Different colors, see?

If you pay attention, you can learn how to do things right. You don't have to have a perfect family to pay attention.

"Why, what did he do?" Melena asks, curious.

"Oh," Stephanie says, "it was awful. He made her give

her oral presentation without any notes. And then he practically accused her of not even reading the book." She is saying all of this as if I'm not even sitting there. She doesn't mean to embarrass me, but I do not like being the center of attention.

"You should sue him," Melena advises. I can't tell if she's serious or not.

"Oh, Melena—you can't go around suing everyone," Ellen says.

"Kara was great," Stephanie says. "She didn't even flinch."

"What book was it?" Ellen asks me, and she tucks a cherry tomato into her mouth.

"*Island of the Blue Dolphins*," I tell her—a little reluctantly.

"I read that," Ellen says around the tomato, nodding her head. "That's an old book. But it's still good."

Ellen has read everything, practically. "Yeah," I say, digging around in my fruit cup for a grape. "It's okay. But you guys are so lucky to be in Mrs. Nelson's class," I add, trying to change the subject—away from *me*.

"Oh, I don't know," Melena objects, pleating her straw paper. "It's not like she's so easy."

"Well, but she doesn't call you a liar in front of the whole class, anyway," I point out.

Uh-oh, I've accidentally brought the subject back to what a goof-up I am.

46

"And Mr. Benito made Kara miss break," Stephanie continues. "She didn't even have a chance to get a drink of water or go to the bathroom."

Melena shakes her head slowly. "You should have told him you were having your period," she says. Her voice is low, but she is grinning.

"Melena!"

"Jeez, lower your voice," Stephanie says, looking around in case somebody is eavesdropping.

Melena giggles. "Well, okay, but that works. Especially if you have a man teacher. That's why *you* guys are the lucky ones."

I push my tray away. "I could never say that to Mr. Benito," I announce, "even if it was the truth. I'd rather just curl up on the floor and die."

"I can't even tell him when I have to go to the bathroom for—for the regular reasons," Stephanie says, blushing. "In fact," she adds, "I don't think girls should even have to *have* men teachers."

"Oh, I don't know. I can ask Mr. Benito if I can use the bathroom if there aren't any boys around," I say. I am thinking of Howard when I say this. Howard likes to pinch his nose shut and yell, *Hurry, hurry!* when he hears a girl ask if she can please be excused. He is *so* immature.

"This is gross," Ellen announces. She can be very ladylike, but she's not stuck-up about it, so that's okay.

"Yes," Stephanie says, making her funniest prissy face.

"You girls are just disgusting! Talking about *those things*. And at lunch, too."

And then we all laugh. I laugh the most, though, because we aren't just talking about me anymore.

I mean, everyone has to go to the bathroom, don't they?

Chapter Five

Never-Ending Thursday

Last Halloween my mom was busy fighting with my dad, but the Halloween before that she spent in bed. She was there almost the whole month, really. Those times were always hard on my mom but easier on me and my dad.

I shouldn't admit it, but it's true.

It was a hot October in Pasadena that year, and I would walk home from school past decorated houses that seemed to be trying hard to pretend it really was fall. Uncarved pumpkins sat embarrassed on sunny front porches, hunky strands of fake cobwebs wrapped dusty bushes together, and cardboard skeletons grinned out at me from inside living room windows.

Not at our house, though. At our undecorated house, the morning paper would still be lying half-open in the driveway, yellowing and brittle, providing shade for a few dizzy ants. That was my clue: Mom had not gotten out of bed.

"Kara? Is that you?" she'd call out, her voice weak. "Come on upstairs, honey," she'd say, and I'd grab a couple of diet sodas and start climbing.

Our house has the half bathroom downstairs, and one bedroom that used to be an office. My dad was sleeping there off and on that year; he kept the sofa bed unfolded all the time. You could barely walk across the room, it was so crowded.

Our house also has three upstairs bedrooms—one for me, one for my mom, and one for all her extra stuff. She can't throw anything away. The stairwell is lined with old framed pictures of relatives I never knew. I don't think even my mom and dad know who they are.

The light in the stairwell was burned out all that fall, but no one replaced it. Well, Dad hardly ever went upstairs— maybe he didn't realize. Anyway, up I would climb.

"Kara?"

"I'm coming, Mom." Her room was dark. You could barely see her under the covers.

This was the worst part of the day for me, because my mom would feel so bad about everything. I was always the first one to start crying, though. I almost hated her for that.

"I'm a terrible mother," she said one day.

"Oh, Mom, no you're not," I told her.

"Yes I am. I didn't even make you a snack. And I don't have the slightest idea what to give you and your father for dinner."

"Dad always makes dinner anyway," I mumbled.

"What? What did you say?"

"Nothing. Want to watch TV?"

"God, no," my mom said, reaching for her soda. She knocked the can over and then tried to mop up the mess with wads of pink Kleenex that smelled like baby powder. I ended up doing it for her. "I'm hopeless," she said.

"Oh, Mom—no you're not," I told her.

"Hopeless and fat," she said, lifting the covers and peering down at her skinny self as if she'd suddenly turned into Sausage Lady.

"No, that's me," I said, trying to make a joke.

"No wonder people laugh at me," she said, not even listening. "I make myself sick."

"You look pretty, Mom," I said, trying to make her feel better. "Really, you do. You're beautiful!"

And then I was the one who reached for one of those baby powder Kleenexes.

That was about the time I discovered Island of the Blue Dolphins....

HOW TO BLEND IN

1. **Never be first in line for anything, or sit in the front row in class, or raise your hand before someone else does**—even if you know the right answer. Spell a word wrong in spelling bees so you won't have to stand there in front of everyone. Not so fast that the teacher gets suspicious, though—just fast enough.

2. **Keep your eyes and ears open and your mouth shut, in fact.**

3. **Pay attention when you go over to someone else's house.** See how they do stuff—then do stuff that way. No one will know you aren't real.

4. **Same thing when you watch TV or look at magazines.** Even the commercials can teach you a lot. I think life would be perfect if you could live the way they do in commercials.

The first time I read *Island of the Blue Dolphins*, I thought the whole thing sounded really cool. I wished I could be on the island with Karana. I'd keep her company. We were so much alike, I thought—even our names were almost the same.

The second time I read the book was one of those

periods when my mom was staying in bed, my dad was staying at his office, and I was staying in my room most of the time. I didn't think about Karana as much as I had the first time—I thought about the island. It was as if I were *already* on that island. Nobody knew just how weird my family really was—and that made me feel lonely.

That's when I started calling it Lonely Island.

The third time I read the book, it was summer, and my mom had just thrown a hissy fit because she thought I hadn't asked permission to go to the library. Actually, I *had* asked permission—only it was from my dad, who said yes, but was conveniently gone when the hissy fit happened. My mom and dad were fighting then, and I didn't want to get my dad into more trouble, so I didn't say anything about having gotten his permission.

She grounded me for two days.

Enough time for a good read. Thanks, Mom.

This time, though, I had a different feeling about the book. I could escape to Lonely Island whenever I wanted to, I realized—by picking up the book.

Later on, I didn't even have to open it. I could put myself on that island just by thinking about it, I knew every bluff and cove so well.

Parents fighting? Mom out of control? *Lonely Island.*

Grover stressing me out? *Lonely Island.*

Lonely? *Lonely Island*—but you're *supposed* to be lonely on a deserted island.

Basically, what I did was to change my thinking about what it meant to be lonely. I changed it into something good.

When you're alone, for instance, no one can ignore you or hurt your feelings. You don't have to tell anyone you're having a great day when you aren't. You only have to take care of yourself. You don't have to worry about other people all the time—you get to think about yourself for a change.

You don't have to keep secrets. No one can disappoint you.

For me, taking a quick trip to Lonely Island became the way I made things better—even when there were tons of people around. I could put myself there in the blink of an eye. That's what I meant when I said that the book saved my life.

Bad things happen on the island, sure, but they happen for logical reasons. For long, restful minutes I can watch otters float blissfully on ocean swells. I see gulls hang suspended in the air and the tightness eases in my throat. I feel the wind blow crayon-yellow wild mustard flowers against my bare legs and I know that I am home.

No one can find me there.

Mr. Benito gives me a funny look after lunch. I guess he found the little piece of paper with the word *Karana* on it. I give him an empty look back, though, telling him that he and I do not have anything special to say to one another.

It was exactly like that with Karana in the book. She could speak no words to the village elders. *They* were the ones who decided the people had to leave the island, by the way. And everyone left—everyone except Karana and her brother.

Okay.

I'll give *you* the book report, because that's not the same as telling the story out loud to a bored sixth-grade class. Here is what happened to Karana: First, her little brother was killed by wild dogs soon after they were abandoned. After that, she was alone. Karana would stand on the headland, which is like a cliff, and search the ocean for signs of the ship that she hoped would come back to rescue her—to save her from being alone.

No ship.

She only made two friends in all the time she was on the island, and she was there for eighteen years. Eighteen years! The first friend was a wild dog named Rontu, the leader of the wild dog pack. She killed a bunch of the dogs, and she almost killed Rontu, but then she decided to tame him instead.

That is hard to understand, especially since it was the dogs who killed her brother. Maybe that just goes to show how lonely she was.

Rontu probably made Karana feel more real, that's what I think. See, we really are alike.

A long time later she secretly made friends with Tutok, a girl who came to the island with some Aleut hunters, who had become the fierce enemy of Karana's tribe, but it was only for a few days. When she first heard the other girl speak, it sounded funny to her—because she hadn't heard any words spoken for so long.

I know what that feels like! But kind of in a different way. For some reason, my mother has to talk-talk-talk to me—or *at* me, really—when I get home from school. And I mean it, she really *has* to, even when she can't get out of bed except to go to the bathroom. It's as if talking to me is her one job now.

Listening to my mother talk is one of the ways I take care of her.

She likes to tell me what's what, because she's been saving up all day. But after that, nothing. From before dinner to when I say good-bye at my mother's door the next morning, silence—except for the TV in her room, and that's not the same.

So when Stephanie says, "Hi, Kara!" in the morning, those words sound brand-new to me.

I did get to talk to my father in private one time. Mom was in the shower and she didn't hear the phone ring. I could tell that my dad wanted to ask me something. Finally, he did. "Kara, your mother's still taking her medicine, isn't she?" See, my mom is supposed to take these pills that kind of smooth out both the bad times and the scary-happy ones.

"Yeah," I told him. "She complains about it, but she's still taking the pills. I count them every so often." I don't tell him that the reason I do this is because she has been acting so weird. Like I said before, what could he do about it? Things would only get worse if I told. And she *is* taking her medicine—I think.

But she might be flushing the pills down the toilet for all I know.

"You'd tell me if there was anything wrong, wouldn't you?" my dad asked. I could figure out what he wanted the answer to be.

"Sure," I said.

I wish we still had Feather. Feather could be like Rontu for me if she still lived at my house. Well, not really, because Rontu was smart and brave, and Feather was kind of a nervous wreck—from all the yelling last fall, when my mother and father were fighting so much. Feather would tuck her tail down so you couldn't even see it, her back legs would shiver, and sometimes she would hide. I found her in the shower once. I almost crawled in next to her.

Even though she was a nervous wreck, though, Feather would have kept me company. We could have been nervous wrecks together.

"Ms. Biggs?" Mr. Benito is saying. "Would you care to join the discussion?"

Uh-oh. I have not been keeping my eyes and ears open.

But whenever a teacher asks if you would care to join the discussion, the answer is always *yes*. "Uh, sure—yes," I say, and I try to look alert.

"We were talking about how to improve the city bus system," Mr. Benito says. Our class has these discussions sometimes. They're not so much about the bus system or fast food or TV, Mr. Benito says, as they are about being able to make a case for something or argue against it.

"Jenna thinks that there should be seat belts on the city buses," he adds, nodding toward Jenna Haller, a quiet girl who sits over by the window. She blushes because he just said her name. "And Marta was just telling us that she thinks the fare should be raised," Mr. Benito continues.

"That way, there won't be so many poor people riding on the bus," Marta points out. "They make it all crowded and dirty," she adds, making a face.

You're not supposed to just say, *Wow, what a dumb idea!* in these discussions, so I say, "Well, the buses here don't seem that dirty to me." Which they don't. Pasadena buses are okay, for buses.

"Hah," Marta says, raising her hand. "Would you eat off the floor on one?"

"Marta, wait until I call on you," Mr. Benito says. "Kara? Do you want to answer that question?"

"I wouldn't eat off the floor no matter where I was," I say. *Not like some people*, I add—but only to myself. A couple of kids snicker as though they could hear what I was thinking, and Marta glares at me.

Howard raises his hand halfway. "But what are poor people supposed to do if they can't afford to ride the bus anymore?" he asks when Mr. Benito calls on him.

"Ride in their limos," this boy named Scott says, and a lot of kids laugh.

"Wait your turn, Scott," Mr. Benito says. "Were you finished, Howard?"

"Yeah," Howard says, "except that poor people need to use the bus to get to work. They'll just get poorer if they can't work."

I think I like Howard a little better now.

Marta's hand flies up into the air again. "Marta?" Mr. Benito says, sighing a little.

"Poor people don't even *want* to work, my father says," she informs the class. "It's like with homeless people. It's their own fault they're that way—so we don't have to feel sorry for them, my father says."

"What about the homeless people who are mentally ill?" Mr. Benito asks. "Is it their own fault they're that way?"

Mentally ill! I feel dizzy, almost as though I am going to faint.

I do *not* want our class to talk about people who are mentally ill.

I lean into the wind and struggle up the path to the highest bluff on the island. The sun makes the top of my head prickle with perspiration, but I want to see if the elephant seals are back yet. I want to find out if—

I am trying hard, but I cannot erase a terrible picture that has jumped into my mind. It is of my mother, smelling bad and dressed in raggedy clothes, striding up and down the aisle of the bus, telling everyone what's what. She stumbles up to Marta Heinz. . . .

This could happen someday, I have to admit it. It's up to me to make sure that it doesn't.

Listen, my mom has always been a little strange, a little different from other mothers, ever since I can remember. Daddy told me once that she got sick right after he first met her in college. Not *sick* sick, just — really sad. Extremely sad, I guess. I don't know.

Maybe she's kind of, like, *allergic* to us. Things definitely got worse after I was born, anyway.

So I owe it to my mom to take care of her.

I guess my mom's strangeness is why I started noticing how other people did things. I wanted to be more like them—and less like her. But it's hard to tell the difference between someone being a little strange and being a *lot* strange while that change is happening. Especially when the person changing is your very own mother.

I said before that watching my mom used to be like watching a surfer, but since Christmas, it's been more like watching a person who is walking over a bridge—like the one at Disneyland that leads to Sleeping Beauty's castle. Only this bridge is invisible. That is exactly the way I picture it.

And the big question is, when do you say that a person is on the other side of an invisible bridge? Even though she still takes her pills, I think my mom crossed over the bridge after my dad left last December. But she did it little by little, so it was hard to tell that it was happening. And now, nobody knows it happened but me.

My dad doesn't know.

The neighbors don't know.

My school doesn't know.

My mom sure doesn't know.

But I can handle it.

Because if people can change one way, they can change the other way, right? That's the number-one-important thing! It's just a question of me keeping things the same until my mom has a chance to turn around and walk back over the bridge.

And then things will be normal again.

"Crazy people could get help if they really wanted to," Marta is saying. "They can take pills."

Pills. I wish there *was* a pill that would really help my mom, not like the ones she's taking now. I would slip that magic pill into her microwaved macaroni-and-cheese dinner and hope like anything that she didn't see it— because if she saw it, she'd think *I* was against her, too.

She already thinks that now, a little.

"Kara?" Mr. Benito is asking. "Do you have anything to add?"

"No," I tell him. "Like I said, I think the buses are pretty clean already. They're okay. Basically, I mean."

Chapter Six

Thursday Continues

My birthday is September 17, and so my eleventh birthday was just six weeks before that bad Halloween. Mom wasn't staying in bed all day then—in fact, she couldn't sleep. She didn't want to eat much, either. She was worried about food all the time. Too much fat, too many chemicals, whatever. My dad and I stopped listening to her after a while.

So she didn't eat and couldn't sleep. What <u>did</u> she do? She prowled around the house all night. It was creepy. Once, I woke up in the middle of the night and she was just standing there in the dark, looking at me.

Okay.

My mom usually looks pretty good—she's skinny, and she has long black hair that she lets get sort of wild—but she looked terrible that September. Big shadows under her eyes, and a jumpy little muscle there, too. Unwashed hair, unbrushed teeth. Wringy hands. You get the picture.

So anyway, my dad got this "wonderful idea" that I should have a birthday party—or at least invite a friend over to spend the night.

(Ha, ha.)

I could just see it. We wake up at two A.M., and there she would be, folks, standing there—The Prowler.

Like I could live <u>that</u> down.

But my dad gets that way sometimes—as if he can make something be the way he wants it to be just by acting as though nothing is wrong.

"Maybe next year I'll give a party," I told him, pretending to think it over. "I'd really rather go out to dinner with you and Mom this year. And we could go to a movie," I added, to make him feel better.

So that's what we did—me and my dad, anyway.

Because finally, two hours before we were supposed to leave, my mom started sleeping. And sleeping.

It's as though she wanted to sleep straight through my celebration—such as it was.

HOW TO FOOL YOUR OWN BEST FRIEND

1. **Learn how to tell a sideways lie.** That's like when your friend asks you a question and you change the subject, or give the answer to a different question. It's not as bad as a real lie, the kind you have to tell other people.

2. **Learn not to feel too bad about telling sideways lies.** You are doing your friend a favor if the truth would only upset her.

"My mom wants to know, can you come over to our house this afternoon? And stay for dinner?" Stephanie asks me during our last break of the day.

"My mom is sick, Steph—remember?" I tell her. See? I've changed the subject.

"Well, yeah," Stephanie says, "only if she's sick, what difference does it make? We just got a new barbecue, and it's warm enough to cook outside—according to my dad, anyway. This will be our first time since we moved here. And you can bring some food back to your mother."

A late February cookout! That's strange, even for Pasadena. I *can't* go over to Stephanie's, though. My mom

65

would freak if I wasn't *right there*. What if she needed me for something? "It gets dark so early," I say, sideways.

"Our patio has outside lights," Stephanie answers, as if she was prepared for this objection. Her forehead wrinkles up, and even her springy black hair looks ready for a fight.

I don't know why this particular invitation is so important to Stephanie. After all, I've said no to her a dozen times since she moved in—usually when she asks if she can come over to *my* house. "We have school tomorrow," I say, answering a different question. It's like playing checkers.

"My mom says we're going to have an early dinner," Stephanie answers. "We can work on our homework in the afternoon." She puts her hands on her hips.

I *know* that I won't be able to go to Stephanie's house this afternoon, but maybe—*maybe*—I can sneak away for dinner, especially if it's an early one.

The very idea is like having the sun go up in my heart.

Maybe I can do it!

But I don't know.

"Are those new shoes?" I ask Stephanie, changing the subject big-time. She has this thing about shoes.

Stephanie holds out a foot, a pleased look on her face as she examines it. She is wearing a kind of sandal-shoe, and she bends her foot first this way, then that way. The wrinkle in her forehead is almost gone. "They're *almost* new," she says. "Do you like them?"

"Yeah, I do," I say, peering down.

"You don't think they make my feet look too big?" Stephanie asks, putting her foot back on the ground. "Be honest."

I tilt my head and narrow my eyes. "No," I finally say. "But your white sneakers do sometimes."

"Oh, I know," Stephanie exclaims. "I feel like I'm walking around with big old boxes on my feet."

"Well, but sneakers are comfortable," I point out, settling into an old discussion—which is usually good for at least five minutes.

"*Comfortable!*" Stephanie says with predictable scorn. Stephanie has this theory that *comfortable* is just for old people. She says it's our duty as kids to do things with style.

Style.

I wonder how stylish she'd think my mother is?

My mother, who won't use deodorant anymore—much less perfume, which lots of moms use every day—because she says there's no one to wear it for.

My mother, who hasn't changed out of her old flannel nightgown for the last three days.

Would Stephanie still like me if she saw the way my mother is now?

"You changed the subject again," Stephanie scolds me.

Uh-oh—busted.

Steph tugs the hem of her pink turtleneck until it is

lying perfectly smooth. "You're always doing that. But what about it? Can you come over or not? You know you *want* to," she adds, teasing suddenly.

I think for a second. It's true, I've liked going over to Stephanie's house the few times I've been there—mostly on weekend mornings. In fact, I've *loved* it. Her mom and dad are really nice, and they have a cat, too—named Scarlett.

"My mom can call your mom if you want," Stephanie coaxes me.

"No!" I exclaim. "I mean, that wouldn't be such a good idea," I say, trying not to sound so upset.

"But why not?" Stephanie asks me, irritated once more. "If my mom—"

"Just—no, okay?" I interrupt her. "Let me handle this my own way. If my mom is asleep when your mom calls, she'll really be mad. She just hates it when someone wakes her up."

Stephanie grins suddenly, surprised. "So does that mean you're coming?" she asks.

"Not in the afternoon, but maybe I can come for dinner," I tell her.

Maybe for dinner. That sun is up now—and it's a Pasadena sun, not a Lonely Island sun.

Stephanie doesn't know what a big deal this is for me, to even *think* I can get away for dinner. I haven't left my house for dinner since Christmas, not counting Valentine's Day weekend, when I stayed with my dad.

But I ought to be able to do stuff, right? To do the things that real people do? Anyway, the time my mother *needs* me to be there is right after school. I almost never see her again after I bring her dinner up to her bedroom. She won't even know that I'm gone—if I actually go, that is.

"Well, I guess dinner is better than nothing," Stephanie says. "When will you know for sure whether you can come or not?"

"When I'm knocking on your door," I say. It sounds as though I'm joking.

It's no joke, though.

"Kara?" Mr. Benito says just as class lets out for the day. "Could you come up here for a moment?"

My eyes zoom to the clock. I have only eighteen minutes to get home. I trot up to his desk. "Yes?" I say. "I'm sorry, but I'm kind of in a hurry. I—I have a dentist appointment," I flat-out lie.

"I called your house at lunchtime," Mr. Benito says, looking troubled. "I wanted to talk with your mother or father about us having a conference."

I cannot listen to this. What has he done to me?

I am standing on the headland looking out to sea. The sun is setting, the wind blows stinging-hard on my sunburned face, and dry grass whips against my ankles.

69

Above me, seagulls hover on the wind and cry like babies, their red mouths hanging open. Far below, waves roll soundlessly into the empty cove.

Wave after wave after wave.

And I am somewhere in the middle, suspended between sea and sky.

"Kara, did you hear what I said?" Mr. Benito is asking.

"But you told me you wouldn't call," I finally manage to say.

"I changed my mind," Mr. Benito tells me. "I got to thinking about it, and I realized that the notes I send home with you have a way of disappearing. Then I get distracted until it's time to send home another note, then another."

Hey, that's what I've been counting on.

My heart is pounding. Above the roar in my ears, I hear the classroom clock give another *click*. Three more minutes have lurched by. "So what did she say?" I ask Mr. Benito.

"Well, I'm not sure that I even got the right number," he tells me, frowning. "The woman I spoke with seemed to think I was a bill collector or a doctor or something. She seemed very angry, Kara. Could that have been your aunt?"

"Maybe," I tell him. "What number did you call?"

Mr. Benito slides a piece of paper across his desk. My phone number is on it.

"That's wrong," I tell him, which is another lie—the straight-ahead kind again.

"But I got it from school records," he objects.

"Then the school records are wrong. That's supposed to be a seven," I lie, pointing to the last number.

"Are you sure? Because the woman I spoke with finally admitted that she has a daughter who is a student at Maybeck Middle School. But she said she'd call the police if I didn't stop pestering her—and then she hung up on me."

"Well, it sounds a little like my aunt," I lie again, "but it couldn't have been, because you dialed the wrong number. Don't worry, though. I'll bring your note home, and then my mother or my father will call you."

Sure they will.

Mr. Benito taps his lower lip with his finger, which is what he does when he is worried.

"I don't know, Kara. I think—"

"Look," I interrupt, "I have to go now, or our housekeeper will be really worried. So will my aunt."

For this to happen today, of all days! I'll never be able to sneak out of the house tonight if my mom is all in an uproar.

"Good-bye," I say, and I whirl around—almost skidding on the floor. I regain my balance and lean down. I pick up a scuffed-up scrap of paper.

On it, underneath the footprints, the word *Karana* is printed firmly and neatly.

He never even saw it.

I'm glad. It serves him right, calling my house like that!

"Good-bye," I say again.

I scoop up my backpack, and I flee.

Running, running, running along the broadest beach on Lonely Island. . . .

My unstylish sneakers pound on the sidewalk, and I can feel my teeth clack together with each stride as I head for home. I pass little groups of kids who are waiting for rides or just hanging out together. Someone—maybe it's Stephanie—calls out, "Hey, Kara!" but I ignore whoever it is.

It's funny to be hurrying when I'm rushing home to crazy-time. But for now, that's what I have to do—and tonight, at least, I have something to look forward to.

Freedom. This is my promise to myself.

I *am* going to sneak out of the house and have dinner with Stephanie and her family.

It is exactly the kind of thing that a real person would do.

Chapter Seven

Thursday Afternoon

Things were going pretty great with my mom when I turned ten, so I actually <u>did</u> have a birthday party that year. My birthday was on a Saturday, which is the most perfect day of all to have a party. And I invited two girls—Alice and Ginny—from my fourth-grade class to go see a movie in the afternoon and then go out to this place that is just like a real Fifties diner. My mom and dad came, too, but they sat somewhere else during the movie and let us have our own table when we ate. I think I even saw them holding hands when we were at the diner!

That was the most real I ever felt—first, because everyone was happy, and second, because there were witnesses.

Alice transferred to private school the next year, and Ginny moved away. Maybe they don't even remember that party. <u>Probably</u> they don't. But I remember it.

I had fun.

When we got home that night, Mom wanted to tuck me

in. "You're so old now—I know you don't need me to do this," she told me, "but I need me to do this. S'okay?"

"S'okay," I said, and she pulled the covers up to my chin. Then she curled up next to me in the dark and stroked my bangs back from my forehead. It felt so good.

"You're a terrific kid," she whispered. "You do know that, don't you?"

That's a hard kind of question to answer, so I just said, "I guess." I wanted her to keep on talking, though.

"I couldn't have invented a better kid," she said, drawing her finger lightly down the bridge of my nose as if she had just finished sculpting it.

"I couldn't have invented a better mom," I told her, because—oh, I don't know. Not only to be polite, though. I meant it, because she can't help it if she's sick, can she? When she is able to, she takes good care of me. And she loves me all the time.

I think my mom is very courageous. It must be scary being her.

Mom's breath seemed to catch in her throat, and she gave me a little hug and buried her head in the crook of my neck. "Oh, Kara," she said, her voice muffled, "I don't know what I ever did to deserve a daughter like you. Somebody gave me a break the day you were born, that's all. I'm just so sorry that I—"

"Don't be sorry about anything," I interrupted her, trying not to cry. "You're perfect, Mom."

74

"No, you're perfect."

"No, <u>you</u> are," I said, and then we both started giggling.
Giggling—and crying.

HOW TO SURVIVE LISTENING TO YOUR MAYBE-CRAZY MOTHER

1. **Agree with whatever she says.** Don't argue, whatever happens.

2. **If she starts in on you, change the subject to something she loves to gripe about**—like doctors, carjackings, or chemicals in the food.

3. **Your expression should be interested-looking, and you should learn how to make agreement noises.** Not words, just noises.

4. **But find something you can listen to inside your head while she is talking.** I don't use the island for that, though—she might be able to tell what I'm thinking. Instead, I use the song "John Jacob Jingleheimer Schmidt."

5. **Tell yourself that pretty soon it will be over.** No one can talk forever, even if it seems that way.

"Where *were* you?" my mom asks. She is standing in the middle of her bedroom, the telephone receiver in her hand. She must have washed her hair, because it is standing out from her head like a scary black halo. I can hear the phone *beep-beep-beep*, the way it does when you accidentally knock it over.

"Mom! You didn't call the police, did you?" I ask, rushing over to her. Because, like I said before, she doesn't know it, but if the police ever come to our house, *she's* the one they'll be taking away.

I hold out my hand.

My mother smells bad, like cigarette smoke with something sour mixed in. The leafy shampoo smell coming from her hair only makes me notice the bad smell more.

"No, but I will call them next time—I swear to God!" she says, breathless.

"I'm sorry, Mom," I tell her, my voice as soothing as I know how to make it. "You don't have to swear to God." I keep my hand outstretched, hoping that she will give me the phone, because I can't fight her for it. She seems to have gotten stronger and stronger lately, even though she barely eats a thing.

She looks down at my hand, suspicious. "Did you wash yet? Your school is probably crawling with germs. *Kids*," she adds, disgusted.

She's got some nerve. I hate my mom.

No, I love her.

"I'll do it now," I tell her. "Look, look, I'm going into the bathroom. Just hang up the phone, okay?"

I watch her in the bathroom mirror as I scrub my hands with the strongest antibacterial soap you can buy without working in a hospital. It is bright blue and practically glows in the dark. My mother has it delivered from the pharmacy, along with her pills. She finally *does* hang up the phone, and she goes back to bed, taking it with her. She cradles it like a baby.

Her bed is like the nest of some big sloppy animal. The sheets and blankets seem to be swirled into a kind of whirlpool, one that doesn't move.

"Did you eat anything today?" I ask her after drying my hands on a damp towel. I already know the answer to this, though, because I saw the cereal box in the kitchen trash. My mother still trusts cereal for some reason—probably because the TV ads show cartoon vitamins pouring into the box, just before the box is sealed and closed tight. She's big on vitamins.

And me—she still trusts me most of the time.

"Why do you always want to know if I ate anything?" she asks. "Is someone telling you to ask me that? Like your *father?*"

"No," I say, shaking my head. "I promise, Mom."

"Swear to God?"

I try to hide my sigh. "Okay," I say, holding up one

hand, "swear to God." I drag a chair up to the side of her bed.

My mom watches me sit down, and then a pleasant look settles on her face. This is a good time, almost—the time when she pretends that she is just like other moms. "So, how was your day?" she asks, sounding as normal as anything.

This is our routine.

"It was okay," I tell her, as if I am reading from a script.

"How's Stephanie?" she asks.

"Fine," I say. I don't say anything about going over to her house for dinner, of course. In fact, I try to put the thought of it out of my head, because my mother is kind of spooky. It seems as though sometimes she can tell what is on your mind.

And going to dinner at Stephanie's house has begun to seem as though it's the most important thing in the world that I could do.

"How was lunch?" she asks, her voice singsong.

"Fine," I say. "We had burritos."

"*Mexican* food," she snaps.

Uh-oh. The good time is over. "I had to give an oral presentation today," I say, trying to change the subject. "Mr. Benito—"

"That *foreigner*," she interrupts.

"Mom," I say, even though I should know better, "he isn't foreign. He was born in Whittier." A hopeless feeling settles over me—kind of like stepping into a too-hot

78

shower on a too-warm day. But at least it doesn't sound as though she knows it was Mr. Benito who called this afternoon.

"I—think—I—know—about—foreigners," she says as she punches her pillows, trying to get them into a more comfortable position. She flops back onto them, glares at me, and lights a cigarette.

And that is another reason why I can't ever let Mr. Benito call my house again. My mom is convinced that he's a foreigner—when, really, even his *grandparents* were born in Whittier. He told us once.

It is impossible to explain your family to people at school, and it is impossible to explain people at school to your family.

She'll be yelling at *me* next, if things go the way they usually do. I give it five minutes, tops.

John Jacob Jingleheimer Schmidt—that's my name, too! I sing to myself. *Whenever I go out, the people always—*

My mother leans forward, as if she is about to tell me a secret. "Someone called this afternoon," she says, blowing out smoke as she speaks. "Right at lunchtime."

Mr. Benito. "They did?" I ask. I want to jump up and turn away so she can't see my face, but I make myself hold still.

"It was a man, Kara—and I think he *knows*."

"Knows what, Mom?"

My mother ignores this question. She looks as stern

as a TV show judge now, in spite of the sagging neck of her cereal-spattered nightgown and her tangled hair. "And you are *not* going to talk back to me, young lady," she says, as if picking up an old argument—one that I missed the start of. "You don't know the first thing about the real world," she adds.

Okay. If I say, *You're right*, she'll tell me that I'm being sarcastic.

If I say, *Yes, I do*, she'll tell me I'm talking back.

If I say the truth—*Well, neither do you anymore!*—she'll . . . oh, who knows what she'll do? Probably explode right before my very eyes.

So I say, "Mmm," and try to look like I'm sorry—sorry for not knowing anything about the real world.

"The real world is a dirty place," she says, leaning forward in bed.

And I can't help it. I am unable to resist escaping to my island.

The devilfish lives in the sea cave at the south side of Lonely Island. She is a danger to me, so I will have to kill her somehow.

I throw my spear. She tries to hide herself by releasing a cloud of black liquid, but the spear has caught! I hold on tight to the sinew rope that the spear is tied to, and she starts to drag me across the rocks and into the salty green water. My hands begin to bleed, but still I do not let go.

This devilfish will scar me for life, probably.

"Kara, are you even listening to me?" my mother is asking. She narrows her eyes.

"Yes, I'm listening," I lie.

I switch back to the song. *John Jacob Jingleheimer Schmidt—that's my name, too! Whenever I go out, the people always shout—*

"Are you *grinning* at me?" my mother asks, really furious now.

"No, Mom," I tell her.

"Because if you think this is *funny*, young lady," she says, ignoring my reply, "you've got another think coming. What in the world is the matter with you?" See, my mother likes to fight when she gets worked up. I think that's the thing that makes *her* feel more real.

"Nothing, Mom. I just—"

"Are you *arguing* with me now?" she asks, and she shakes her head as if she can't believe what she is hearing.

I shake my head, too, as if there is an invisible string connecting us—or a sinew rope, maybe. I have to change the subject, and fast. "Did you see the mail yet?" I ask her. That always gets her. Lately, anyway. Maybe she's afraid my dad is going to write her a letter—or maybe she's afraid he *isn't* going to write her a letter. Because he hasn't written a word.

My mother shrinks back against her pillow. "It's here already?" she asks, her voice a whisper.

"I could bring it up if you want," I offer.

"No," she exclaims. "The *mail*," she says, as if forcing herself to repeat a disgusting word just to prove how strong she is. "Anyone can send whatever hurtful words they want through the mail, Kara. It's not fair."

This really bothers her. I feel bad for bringing up the subject, but only a little.

At least we don't have a slot for mail in our front door. I don't know *what* she'd do then. Nail a board over it, maybe.

"It's probably just bills," I say.

She seems to collapse onto her pillow again. "I can't cope with the mail, Kara. Can't you see how tired I am? I never used to be this tired," she tells me. "I used to be fun. We used to have a lot of fun, your father and I."

Notice who she leaves out.

She's about to start crying, I just know it—and then I will start crying, too.

"Mmm," I say. I grit my teeth, and I get ready to give her a comforting hug.

Whenever I go out, the people always shout, "There goes John Jacob Jingleheimer Schmidt!" Da-da-da-da-da-da-da-DA.

Chapter Eight

Thursday Fun!

The further back I try to think, the more things blur to-gether. How old was I the year Mom tried to quit smoking? Or the year she threw such a bad temper tantrum in our favorite restaurant that to this day we have never gone back? Or the year she decided my dad didn't love her anymore?

I was nine that year, I think.

It's a funny thing about her feeling that way, though, because when I was nine, my dad did still love my mom—I'm just about positive. I was in third grade then, in Ms. Harris's class, and they came to family night together. I saw my dad looking at her while she was busy writing down just about every word Ms. Harris was saying. It was as if she was trying to be the best mother in the whole wide world.

He couldn't stop watching her, and there was love in his eyes.

My dad is handsome, I think—tall, with blue eyes like

mine and light brown hair he cuts real short—but he looked tired even then.

He kept telling her he loved her all that year, in fact, but she kept saying stuff like "You'd be better off without me," and "I don't know why you put up with me." It's almost as if she _made_ him stop loving her.

Maybe he got worn out, I don't know.

~~~~~~~~~~~~~~~~~~~~~~~~

HOW TO SNEAK OUT OF THE HOUSE AT NIGHT

1. **I have never done this before now, so I can't write down any plan that will work for everyone.** In _my_ case, all I have to do tonight is to walk out the door, _quietly,_ because my mom never checks up on me anyway. While I'm awake, at least.

2. **If I get caught, I will have to figure out a better way to sneak out at night**—because I've decided that a real person cannot stay alone in her room for the rest of her life! And then I will have a system, and I'll tell you all about it. So you will be the second to know.

~~~~~~~~~~~~~~~~~~~~~~~~

Okay.

After my mom finishes "having a conversation" with me, which as usual takes about an hour and a half, I heat up a frozen dinner for her in the microwave—gray Swedish meatballs on noodles tonight, with elderly-looking little peas—and take it up to her room.

Uh-oh, I hope my mom doesn't think her *dinner* is too foreign. I think of all the upsetting, foreign-sounding things I could serve her besides Swedish meatballs. French toast, English muffins.

Danish pastry.

I put the tray down outside her door and knock, then go downstairs as if I was about to eat my own dinner in the kitchen with the little TV on low to keep me company.

But instead, I put some dirty clothes in the washing machine, start it, then sit down and look at the clock. I wait for ten minutes, just in case my mom starts yelling about something.

I wait until it is five forty-five. . . .

Not a peep.

I stuff the key to our house in my pocket and slip out the kitchen door, locking it behind me. I walk down the street to Stephanie's house. I don't have to worry about my mom seeing me from her window, because her bedroom faces the backyard.

With each sidewalk square, my steps get lighter and

lighter. It is as though I started wading heavily through the surf toward shore, and have ended up running on smooth damp sand.

I am practically floating by the time I reach the path to Stephanie's front door. Their cat, Scarlett, is curled up on the doormat, and she rolls over onto her back and wriggles when she sees me. "Hi, kitty-kitty," I say, scratching her butterscotch-colored stomach. She grabs hold of my hand with her paws suddenly, and pretend-bites me.

Stephanie opens the door. "Oh," she says, surprised to see me crouching there. "I was just going to come get you."

"Too late," I say. "I'm already here." I think, *Phew!* because the whole night would have been ruined if Stephanie had rung our doorbell. My mom probably would have thought Steph was a home invader, and it would have taken hours to calm her down.

"Well, come on into the kitchen," Stephanie says, tossing back her curly black hair. I notice she has changed out of her school clothes. I should have changed, too. Next time I will.

"Daddy is in the backyard," Steph tells me. "He's more than halfway done cooking the chicken. We're supposed to set the table. How is your mom?"

"She's feeling a little better," I lie. "She says to say hi."

We walk into the Millers' blue-and-white kitchen. They only moved to Pasadena a little while ago, but everything is already neatly put away. In fact, things seem more settled at the Millers' than they do at our house.

Mrs. Miller is tossing something—coleslaw, I think—in a big wooden bowl. "Hello, Kara," she says. Her face fills up with a smile. She has a little space between her two front teeth that makes her look extra friendly.

"Hi, Mrs. Miller. Thanks for inviting me," I say.

"It's always a pleasure seeing you, honey. Grab the pepper, would you?"

I hoist a tall wooden pepper mill.

"Now give it a few good grinds for me," she says, tilting the bowl.

I twist the top of the pepper mill as if I am taking the lid off a jar, and black pepper sprinkles over the salad. "Is that enough?" I ask.

"Once more," she says.

The cat is winding in and out of my ankles in a figure eight while I help Stephanie's mom with the salad. If Scarlett had a rope attached to her tail, she would have tied my feet together by now.

Stephanie is rattling knives, forks, and spoons. Outside, I can hear the radio voice of someone giving a traffic report, and I smell chicken cooking.

It all seems extremely real, if you ask me.

"Whoa—that's enough," Mrs. Miller is saying with a laugh.

"Oh, sorry," I say, and I put down the pepper mill.

87

"What do you want to drink, milk or juice?" Stephanie asks me.

"What kind of juice?" I feel brave enough to ask.

Stephanie peers deep into the refrigerator. "Red," she finally says.

Red. My mom would have a fit. *Artificial colors! There is nothing that color in nature*, she would announce to the world.

"Juice," I decide, without even asking Steph what she is going to have—because tonight is a night of firsts.

I am putting *me* first, for a change.

"Okay. Grab the salt and pepper, would you?" Stephanie says. I follow her out onto the patio. It is dark outside but, as promised, the Millers' patio is blazing with light.

Mr. Miller is tall and thin with black hair that stands out around his head like exclamation points. His face gleams as he fiddles with the vents of a shiny black kettle barbecue. He waves hello at me, then cautiously opens the barbecue lid and pokes a long metal fork into a piece of meat. He looks like a sorcerer who is not too sure how his spell is working out. "How do you tell when chicken is done?" he asks.

"I don't know," Stephanie says, like she is answering a riddle, "when it stops clucking?" She hands him the salt.

"Ooh, sick," I tell her. But I'm laughing, and so is

Stephanie's father. He sprinkles some salt on the sputtering chicken.

"That's my little girl," he says proudly. Then he looks at the chicken again, a considering expression on his face. "I'll give it a few more minutes," he says. "Just to make sure."

"Don't worry—there's a jar of peanut butter in the cupboard," Stephanie whispers to me.

"Good," I whisper back.

In the dining room I watch Stephanie as she starts to set the table, then I copy her. Place mats, plates. Napkins to the left of the plates, folded part next to the plate. Forks to the right of the napkins.

I feel as though I am watching myself set the table. I'm doing it right, just like Stephanie. At my house, my mom always just puts old jam jars filled with knives, forks, and spoons on the table and tells us to help ourselves. She says it saves time that way.

Saving time is not always such a good thing, I think. Well, it depends on what you're saving it for.

So, knives and spoons to the right of the plates. Glasses just above the knives and spoons.

"There. That looks good," Stephanie says, tilting her head.

"Yeah," I agree.

Dinner at the Millers' house is fun, only I feel a little tired from all the laughing and talking. I guess I'm used to it being quiet when I eat dinner, except for the TV.

Or maybe I'm not really tired. Maybe I'm nervous, thinking about my mom. It's hard to tell the difference between feelings sometimes.

Is my mom okay all alone in the house?

Will she *ever* be okay again, really?

Am I doing the right thing trying to take care of her all by myself?

What if all my hard work has paid off and my mom decides that tonight's the night to be a real mom again? My dream come true, only what if she wanders downstairs to make sure I'm eating a nourishing dinner? She'll find an empty kitchen, and that's all she'll find.

I drag my fork through the peppery coleslaw. Thinking about my mom reminds me of this dumb joke I heard once: *Where does the-little-man-who-isn't-there park his car? In the mirage!*

That's what I could tell my mom later—that I was eating dinner in the mirage.

She might believe me, that's the pathetic part.

"What's so funny?" Stephanie asks.

"Oh, nothing," I tell her. "I'm just having a good time over here, that's all."

"Well, that's better than having a bad time," Stephanie says, looking solemn. Then we both laugh a little.

The sound of glass breaking floats into the Millers' dining room through an open window. "What in the world is that?" Mrs. Miller asks, glancing up from her half-empty plate.

"Want me to go look?" Mr. Miller asks. He starts to get up.

Mrs. Miller narrows her eyes and listens. "It didn't sound like a car accident," she says, "and there are no alarms going off or anything. I guess everything is okay. Kara," she says, changing the subject, "I'm going to pack up some of this dinner for your mom when we're done. I sure hope she's up and about soon, honey."

"She probably will be," I say. "But don't pack too much, okay? Because she only eats a little."

Really, I can't stand the idea of throwing the Millers' good food in the garbage—because no *way* can I put it in our refrigerator. My mom would be sure to find it there.

"I hope I get a chance to meet your dad someday soon," Mr. Miller says to me. He is holding up a charred drumstick as if it is a baton and he is about to lead an orchestra.

"He'll probably be down to get me for a visit in a week or so," I lie. With grownups, sometimes you have to lie. It's a *nice* thing to do, really. One little fib can satisfy them enough so that they will ignore your problems for weeks and weeks.

And weeks.

"Well," Mrs. Miller says, "you be sure and have your mom call me if she needs any help with shopping or anything."

"All right, thanks," I say. "But stores around here deliver."

They do, if you pay them enough—which so far we have been able to do. My dad has seen to that.

"That's nice to know," Mrs. Miller says, and she takes a sip of her iced tea. There is a thoughtful look on her face, and I can tell that she would love to ask me questions about my mom and dad—or maybe just about my mom, I don't know. But she's too polite, or perhaps she just can't figure out where to start.

Time for another little fib. I catch Mrs. Miller's eye. "My mom's hair has almost grown back in," I tell her, keeping my voice soft. Because when ladies on TV shows get sick, their hair usually falls out, and everyone gets really sad about it.

"Oh!" Mrs. Miller says. She looks like someone just slapped her.

Oops—maybe I have gone a little too far. But then I remember my mom, and I'm not sorry anymore. Because my mom still needs me to lie for her.

Just until she can stand on her own two feet again.

And the lie about my mom's hair will probably give us another four or five weeks—*easy*—of being left alone.

I turn to Stephanie. "Let's clean up the kitchen," I say.

Stephanie makes a face at me. "Are you *crazy?*" she mutters at me. She jerks her head toward her room.

"We can listen to music while we work. It'll be fun," I

say. I can't exactly explain it, but I love being in the Millers' kitchen.

"Kara," Mrs. Miller says, "that's really not necessary."

"No," Stephanie says, changing her mind suddenly, "Kara's right—we should clean up. Then maybe we'll make ice cream sundaes for everyone." Her eyes gleam. "But you have to eat whatever we put on them, okay?"

Mr. Miller looks nervous. "As long as it's in the ice cream *family*," he says. "No olives or cat food or anything."

"Oh, all right." Stephanie is smiling big now, and so am I.

"*I* know," Stephanie's mom says. "We can each take a bite of everyone else's sundae. That way, we'll know they're safe."

"Or you can serve up four sundaes, but we get first choice," Mr. Miller suggests.

"*Be* that way," Stephanie says, laughing now. "Come on, Kara. Let's clean up the kitchen so we can start in on the sundaes. I get to pick the music, though."

"*Be* that way," I echo.

Chapter Nine

Thursday, After Dinner

I can't remember much before I was eight—just little bits and pieces of memory, as though I am flipping channels in my head.

Happy time: the Christmas that my mom was okay and I got the Barbie Dream House I wanted so much.

Sad time: the summer when my mom wouldn't stop crying.

Scary time: when my mom said she was tired of living. That's why she had to go into the hospital, Dad said. I was only four then.

I'm tired of living, too, sometimes—does that mean I should be in the hospital?

Because I sure could use a rest.

HOW TO CLEAN UP THE KITCHEN (THE MILLER WAY!)

1. **Start playing some really great music.**
2. **Put all the food away.** Cover up anything that needs covering up.
3. **Scrape leftover food from the plates into the trash.**
4. **Throw away any other garbage.**
5. **Rinse off the glasses, plates, and silverware with hot water.** Put everything into the dishwasher, if you have one.
6. **Rinse the serving bowls out and put them in the dishwasher, if there is enough room.** Or wash and dry them.
7. **Fill the sink with hot, soapy water, and wash all the weird stuff**—such as the barbecue fork, for example. Be careful during this part so you don't stab yourself.
8. **Wipe the counters with a damp dishcloth.**
9. **Sweep the floor.**
10. **Turn off the music.**

"Ooh, ooh, oooh!" Stephanie sings, spinning around on one heel. Her brown eyes are closed. She is holding the broom straw-side-up, as if it is her dance partner. Scarlett streaks out of the kitchen, afraid for her tail.

I swing the wet dishcloth at Stephanie, aiming low. It slops against her bare legs. "Omigosh," she says, her eyes opening wide as she jumps back. "What was *that?*"

"Señor Counter Wiper," I say, holding up the cloth. We are just starting to learn Spanish in school. I haven't told my mother yet, naturally.

Would you?

"Oh, yeah?" Stephanie says. "Well, Señorita Broom will take care of *you!*" And she comes running after me. I scream and try to hide. Then the broom's prickly bristles are poking at my back, right through my striped T-shirt, even though I am cowering behind one of the Millers' kitchen chairs.

"Is everything all right in there?" a voice calls from the dining room.

"Fine," Stephanie and I sing out. Then we face each other, wary as gladiators. I stand up and swing the dish-cloth in a slow, menacing circle over my head.

"I just *dare* you," Stephanie whispers, and I get ready to attack.

"What about my pickle sundae?" Mr. Miller wails from the dining room.

"Don't encourage them, Hal," we hear Mrs. Miller tell

96

him. Then she says, "What on earth is going on down the street?" and I hear the front door open.

"We'd better make the sundaes," Stephanie says to me. "Truce?"

"Well, all right. For now," I tell her.

I get two kinds of ice cream from the freezer, chocolate and strawberry, and Stephanie gets out four clean bowls and spoons. "This is going to be fun," she says, and we start to scoop ice cream into the bowls.

"Remember," I caution her, "let's not make any of the sundaes *too* weird. If your mom and dad are really going to get first choice, we'll just end up having to eat whatever's left."

"Yeah," Stephanie says, "but maybe it's worth the risk."

Stephanie has kind of a reckless streak, it seems. I'd like to have a reckless streak. Maybe it's a harder thing to have, though, if you've had a reckless *life*.

"It's *not* worth the risk," I tell her, picturing cat chow or radishes hidden inside the scoops of ice cream—cat chow or radishes that I might have to end up eating.

"Chicken," Stephanie says to me.

The kitchen door swings open, surprising us. Mrs. Miller walks in from the dining room. "Kara," she says quietly, "I think I'd better walk you home. There's something going on over at your house, honey."

I see the water pull back farther than it ever has before,

97

skinning back over rocks, shells, and small coral reefs. Then
the roaring starts.

I see a flash high in the sky, and I look up to see if the sun
has slipped behind a cloud—but that flash is the towering crest
of a wave.

And a tidal wave bears down on Lonely Island.

It is as though the imaginary wave that I was walking
through on my way over to the Millers' has turned on me,
grown monstrous, and knocked me down.

It's all over.

I look at the ice cream, already puddling brown and
pink in the Millers' pretty glass bowls.

"Come on, sweetie," Mrs. Miller says gently.

"No, that's all right," I tell her. "I'll just go alone."

Because I truly am alone now, and I'd better get used
to it.

Chapter Ten

Thursday Disaster

HOW TO LEAVE A PARTY FAST

1. Just go.

There *is* something happening at my house—something awful. Two cars are parked in front. One is my dad's car, and the other is—a police car.

A police car!

This is all my fault. This is what I get for leaving my mom alone.

Our front door is wide open, and there is a square of empty light on the front porch. I don't see any people.

I am running, running, running down the sidewalk.

As I cut across the lawn to get to the front door, two figures appear in the light, my dad and a policeman. They
both look relieved to see me.

"Kara! Thank heavens you're all right," Dad calls out,
and he drops to his knees and wraps me in a gigantic hug.
I hug him back with stiff arms. From upstairs, I can hear
my mom's voice and another woman's voice, too. To my
relief, my mom sounds all right. I mean, she's not yelling
or anything, just arguing.

My father draws back to look me up and down. There
is a cut on his forehead—a bright little zigzag that looks
as if it was drawn on with a red marker. "I'm okay, Daddy,"
I say. "Really. What happened to your head? And what are
you *doing* here?" I ask him. I glance up at the policeman,
feeling shy. And embarrassed. And scared.

Is he going to arrest my mom for something?

And how did my dad's head get cut?

My dad sits down on the step, pulls me down next to
him, then hauls out his handkerchief and pats it against
his cut. "Your teacher called and left a message at my
apartment this afternoon," he says, "but I didn't hear it
until I got home from work. When I tried to call your
mother to talk about it, she—she—" A helpless look
seems to flood his face as he remembers that phone call.

Which I can just imagine. "I didn't know the school
had your new number," I say.

"Kara, of course they have it," he says. "I called them

100

in January right after I got settled. I drove down here as fast as I could," he says—more to the policeman than to me. "And then there was—there was a little problem," he continues, wincing as he pats the cut again, "and I couldn't find you, and I decided I'd better call for some outside help." He nods his head toward the policeman. "His partner is up there with your mother."

"Tell him he'll have to wash his hands first!" My mom's voice floats down from her bedroom. A voice gives some calm reply, but I can't make out the words.

"Where were you?" my dad asks, sounding angry now. "It's almost eight thirty."

It is eight thirty on Lonely Island, too, but it is quiet there— except for the waves crashing against the shore. There must be a storm at sea. The otters will have taken shelter in the honey-colored bluffs. The gulls—

"She was with us," a voice behind me says. I turn around, and there are Mr. and Mrs. Miller. Behind them, in the shadows, I see Stephanie. She raises her hand and waves, but she looks doubtful, as though she's not sure that's the right thing to do.

I wave back as if nothing's wrong.

Nothing's wrong, nothing's wrong, nothing's wrong.

I take a breath. "They didn't know about Mom," I tell my dad. "I lied and told them she was sick."

"Honey, she *is* sick," Dad says, half to me and half to the policeman and Mrs. Miller. "I guess she must have stopped seeing her doctor after I left. I know she was still taking her medicine, though—or refilling the prescription, anyway." He doesn't say how he knows that. Maybe the pharmacy told him.

"She *was* taking her pills," I tell him. "I told you, I counted."

He takes hold of my shoulders. "I don't want to scare you, Kara, but an ambulance is on the way. It'll be here any second. Your mother needs to have some special care for a while."

An ambulance. Special care. Now the waves are pounding in my head. I jump to my feet. "No, she doesn't," I tell him, trying to keep my voice steady. "That will only make everything worse, Dad. And I *was* taking special care of her. We were doing great."

"*You* were doing great, Kara," Dad says. "Your mother was getting sicker and sicker. I blame myself," he adds, sounding bitter.

Why do you blame yourself—for leaving us? For letting her give Feather away? I ask these questions silently.

"It's here," the policeman says. I look over my shoulder and see a shiny ambulance pull into the driveway. Its lights are flashing, but there is no siren. Two men hop out of the ambulance. One of them yawns, and then they walk slowly to the back of the ambulance. They open the door and pull out a stretcher with straps on it. Legs with wheels on them slowly unfold to meet the ground and then snap into place. One man reaches into the ambulance and gets out a big metal box. He puts it on the stretcher.

A few neighbors have turned on their porch lights and come outside. Mr. and Mrs. Miller are whispering together. Stephanie just looks shocked.

I turn to my father. "I can't believe you told the ambulance to come," I whisper. "We were doing just fine. Mom's not really sick. She's been a little out of it, that's all. She was about to get better."

"*Out of it?*" Dad explodes. "She's violent! She threw a clock radio at me, Kara, and she broke the window. Why didn't you *tell* me things had gotten this bad?"

"She was just fine—until you surprised her like that. I had it all under control!" I yell. I don't care who hears me now.

The ambulance men are rattling toward us with the stretcher. One of them is chewing gum.

Mrs. Miller turns toward us and clears her throat. "Excuse me," she says, "but maybe it would be better for Kara to come back to our house for a while. Just until..."

Just until, just until.

Just until my mom is hauled off to the loony bin.

"Coming through," one of the ambulance men says, moving past us. His black hair glistens as if there is gel on it. He doesn't even glance our way. I guess he figures if he's not getting paid to look at a person, why bother?

"She's upstairs, on the left. Another officer is with her. Tell her you just scrubbed your hands," the policeman advises them.

"Gotcha," the gum-chewing ambulance man says, grinning a little.

"It's not funny," I say to him, my voice hard. His eyes meet mine for a second and his grin disappears, then the men are working the stretcher up the staircase.

"Mr. Biggs," Stephanie's mother says, reminding my dad that she is still there.

He looks at her, his expression blank. "Oh," he says, and he turns to me. "Kara, why don't you go on home with Mrs.—Mrs.—"

"Miller," Stephanie's mom says, finishing my dad's sentence for him.

"*This* is my home. I live here with Mom," I tell my father—and anyone else who is listening. I move my feet apart a little, as if that will somehow glue me to the porch.

There are lots of voices coming from upstairs now. I hear my mom say, "Who *are* you?" but she sounds mad, not scared. I wait for her to call my name, to cry out to me for help, but she doesn't.

She doesn't.

My father grips my shoulders, one in each hand.

"Kara, please," he says. "Your mother wouldn't want you to see her like this."

To see her like this? Who does my father think is the only person who has been seeing her like this for the last eight weeks?

"Please," Daddy says again. I look at him, and it is as though he is asking me for a hundred things at once.

To go back to the Millers' house.

To tell him how things ever got this bad.

To forgive him.

"Okay, I'll go to the Millers' house — just for tonight," I say, stony-faced, and I turn around and walk away.

Mrs. Miller takes my hand. *Her* hand feels wonderful, strong and warm — and real. Something melts inside me, and tears start to flow. Stephanie runs up beside us. She grabs for my other hand.

And I let her. I let her.

We are all crying now.

"Why didn't you say something?" Mrs. Miller whispers to me later that night when she is tucking me in. I look over at Stephanie, who is pretending to be asleep. Her back is to us, and the only part of her I can see is her black hair poufing up over her sheet. She is holding her breath, I can tell.

Oh, I don't care who hears what anymore. I am tired, and my face feels stiff from so much crying. The back of

Mrs. Miller's hand feels cool and warm at the same time as she strokes damp hair off my forehead.

I remember when my mom did that.

"I'm sorry," I tell Mrs. Miller.

"Sorry? Honey, you don't have to be sorry," she says, still whispering—kind of. "But why didn't you say something?" she asks again. Her eyes look scared, as if a secret this big might somehow reach out and touch *her* family— as if the secret were a germ, maybe. Her eyes flick over to Stephanie.

"Don't worry. Stephanie's happy," I say.

"Oh, Kara—you're breaking my heart." I can't see the friendly space between her two front teeth at all now.

"I'm sorry," I say again, sniffling a little bit.

"Well, honestly," she says, sounding a little exasperated.

"It's just that—I was scared for things to change. I thought my mom would get better if we could only keep going the way we were," I try to explain. "I thought that she would get better. She was taking her pills," I say, sounding like an echo.

Her pills, her pills, her pills. She *was* taking them.

Or was she flushing them after all?

"Where's my dad?" I ask Mrs. Miller.

"He's making sure your mom gets all settled in at the hospital," she says, smoothing my hair back again. "He figured it might take a while, though. He'll be at your house in the morning, if you want to see him. Oh," she adds,

106

scolding herself, "what am I talking about? Of *course* you'll want to see him."

"I guess," I mumble. I think for a moment. *Do* I want to see him? I don't really know the answer to that. "Will I have to go to school tomorrow?" I ask. Because that would be one good thing, at least—if I got to stay home from school.

She shrugs, suddenly looking exhausted, as if she is thinking, *Gee, invite a kid over for an innocent piece of chicken, and what happens?* "Probably it would be for the best. You can touch base with your father before you go," she says.

I don't say anything.

"It would be for the best," she repeats, convincing herself.

"Whatever," I say, turning my head away from her cool-warm hand.

She is breaking *my* heart. I never thought I'd say it, but that's what kindness can do to you.

"Night," I mumble, pretending to be sleepy.

I hear the door click as she leaves the room. Stephanie had better not say anything nice to me, I think, blinking back a few tardy tears that somehow forgot to fall during the last two hours.

"Kara?" Stephanie's voice whispers a few seconds after the door closes.

"What?"

107

Stephanie waits, as if gathering her courage, then asks, "Are you mad at me?"

"No. What do you want?"

"I want to know if you're okay, that's all."

"Well, I'm *not* okay. What do you expect?"

"I don't know," Stephanie says.

The room is quiet for a moment. "Are you going to tell everyone at school?" I finally ask. Marta Heinz will torment me forever about it, I think, and Ellen will have about a million questions if she finds out, and Melena will probably want me to sue someone.

Stephanie sits up fast. "*Kara!*" she says, shocked, as if she cannot believe that I would ask such a horrible question.

"Well, are you?"

"What kind of friend do you think I am? Of course I'm not going to tell everyone. I'm not going to tell *anyone.*"

"Oh, I don't care," I say, exhausted. "What difference does it make if kids find out? It's not like they thought I was so perfect before, is it?"

Stephanie snorts. "There's nothing the matter with *you*, Kara—it's your mom who's sick. But don't worry, I'm not going to be the one to say anything about it."

"Thanks," I say.

The room is quiet again, but it's an easy quiet this time. "Do you think you're going to have to move?" Stephanie asks me.

"I don't know. Probably."

"Because I don't *want* you to move. I want us always to be friends, Kara. I think you're just about the bravest person I ever met."

"I wasn't being brave, I was being stupid."

"No, you weren't. You were trying to help. You didn't know."

"That's true," I say. I think back on everything that has happened in just one day. "Is this still Thursday?" I finally ask.

Steph leans over to peer at her illuminated clock. "Yeah," she tells me, "but just for ten more seconds."

I count to ten. "It's over," I say.

Chapter Eleven

Three Weeks Later: Another Day

HOW TO GLUE YOUR LIFE BACK TOGETHER

1. With most people, pretend that nothing happened.
2. With yourself, don't pretend that nothing happened.

"She'll look a little different," my dad warns me on the ride over to Las Mariposas, where my mom is staying. This will be the first time I've seen her since—well, you know.

This sounds very scary. *Different how?* I want to ask. Instead, I say, "You don't have to tell me that." I start worrying almost immediately, though.

"I just thought you should be prepared."

"Thanks," I say. I look out the car window as if I am bored. My dad is trying to have a conversation with me, I realize. My mom's counselor probably told him to. It makes me feel a little uncomfortable.

I don't know how to act around my dad anymore. He seems as foreign to me as the people in those photographs that line our stairwell. It's as if we have to get to know each other all over again.

Here's a secret: I *wanted* to move to Santa Barbara with my dad last Christmas! I dreamed about it, even, but I couldn't ask. Mom needed me too much.

Now, though? Maybe it's too late for me to be happy there. It's weird being around my dad.

I guess I'm still kind of mad at him.

I have been staying with the Millers, supposedly so that my school year won't be interrupted before spring break. The truth is, I wouldn't mind leaving Maybeck early—if I didn't have to leave Stephanie, too.

Things are not going great at school. Oh, Mr. Benito has been taking it easy on me for a change, but Marta Heinz has obviously figured out that something's up. "Does Kara look different to you?" she asked Howard before class one morning. She tilted her head and looked at me as if I were a potato, or something else that couldn't hear or answer back.

"No," Howard said, not even looking at me. "She looks exactly the same as always."

"I think she looks cleaner," Marta said. "And her clothes are nicer, too. Less wrinkly."

"Why don't you give everyone a break and just be quiet for a change?" I told her. This doesn't sound like such a gutsy thing to say, but no one in our class talks back to Marta Heinz—*no one*. She's that mean. But where did she get off trying to embarrass me in front of other kids?

"What?" Marta asked, outraged. "*What* did you just say to me?"

Howard grinned and flashed me a look of surprise and admiration. "She told you to be quiet," he said conversationally. "I guess she doesn't know you too well."

"Huh," Marta said, flustered, and she flounced away.

Stephanie has been wonderful, though—especially considering that I've been plunked down in the middle of her room for the last three weeks. It is so great having a friend I can finally talk to. I sure can't talk to my father that way.

My dad has driven down to Pasadena every weekend since the ambulance came for my mother. We stay together in our old house. It's kind of like we're guests there together. We are very polite with one another.

I wash my hands with the bright blue antibacterial soap that is still in every bathroom. I ask my dad if he wants me to heat him up a frozen dinner.

S'okay.

Even though my mother is alive and in the hospital, it

is as though she haunts that house. My dad keeps finding bottles of wine and packs of cigarettes squirreled away in the weirdest places. Sometimes I can almost hear her voice call down the stairs, *"Kara, is that you?"*

She haunts the house in good ways, too, though. When I walk through the door, I can practically hear her excited laugh as she holds up her loot from a shopping trip or starts planning some outrageous party.

When I close my eyes at night, I feel her hand stroking the hair back from my forehead.

"...and so I decided to go ahead and get that sofa bed," my dad is saying as he completes a left turn into a parking lot, "even though it *is* covered in orange velvet. It was a great price, and you'll be much more comfortable than you were on the futon. You'll sleep with your eyes closed, I assume!"

A joke. "Heh, heh." I try to laugh.

My dad stops the car so he can give his name to the parking lot guard, who is standing like a toy soldier in his tiny stucco hut. He tilts his head to get a look at me, and I find myself waving at him like a little kid. I make myself stop.

We pass the guard's inspection, and my dad finds a parking spot in the shade. My mom always says he doesn't mind if we have to walk a mile in the sun—as long as the *car* is comfortable. "We have to check in at the front desk," my dad says, "and then I'll be waiting for you in the

113

library so you and your mom can have some privacy."

"Thanks," I say to him. I wish he would stop talking, though, because I am feeling extremely nervous at the thought of seeing my mother again.

I am trying hard not to take that trip to Lonely Island, if you want to know the truth.

My dad tells me that Las Mariposas is the *in* place to go around here if you lose your marbles, although he doesn't put it quite that way. It's very pretty—like a country club, sort of. A country club for sad people.

A country club with an adobe wall all around it.

There are lots of big old trees here, and grass, grass, grass as far as you can see, all perfectly edged and clipped. And there are flowers here, too. "Easy flowers," my mom will sneer—if she still has a sneer left in her, that is.

Petunias, pansies.

My dad signs us both in, gives me a quick kiss good-bye, then disappears down a gleaming hallway.

A nurse leads me out to my mom.

She is sitting in one of the gardens with a couple of other people. They look perfectly normal to me, and so does my mom. I don't know what my dad was talking about.

Well, she does seem *smaller*, in a way. Her hair doesn't spring out as far as usual, and she's not waving her arms around.

But she looks pretty good, that's the thing. A little

114

zonky, but good. "Kara, darling," she says, getting up from a wooden bench that has a brass marker on the back. I try, but I can't make out the name on it. She holds out her arms as if we are at the airport and she has just gotten off a plane.

Knowing Mom, she's probably glad she has an audience.

"Hi, Mom," I say, feeling shy.

"Darling," she says again, wrapping me in a great big hug. "My little baby darling."

"I'm not exactly little," I say, trying to joke. I shrug up a shoulder to wipe away a tear, though.

"Oh, Kara, you're perfect," she whispers—just for me. "This is my daughter," she says, turning to the two other people, who are still sitting there, watching us as if our reunion is the most fascinating thing to happen at Las Mariposas that day.

Which it probably is, come to think of it.

"We'll walk for a bit," she tells them, leading me away. "How's school going?" she asks me. Her voice sounds a little stiff, as though she has just gotten back from the dentist and still has a mouthful of Novocain. She pats up and down the sides of her peach-colored sweatsuit—searching for cigarettes, probably. There aren't any, but she seems okay about it for once. She sighs.

"It's going great," I lie, being careful not to mention Mr. Benito by name—although one of the women my mother

115

has just been talking to looks like the kind of person Mom would describe as a foreigner. Middle Eastern, I think.

Without asking each other whether that's what we want to do, my mom and I sit down underneath a tree and watch the rainbirds water the lawn in front of us. They swing back and forth, ticking and jerking a little as fans of water droplets fly through the air and settle on the grass.

She reaches out and gently turns my head until I am facing her. "Kara, I took my medicine every single day," she tells me, as if this is something she has promised herself she would say. "It's important that you know that. No matter how rotten I felt, and no matter how much I disliked taking those pills, I knew I had to do it. Your father never would have left you alone for a second if he thought I'd stopped doing what the doctor said. You must know that."

I am so glad to hear her say this—I can hardly catch my breath.

"But what went wrong?" I finally ask.

My mom shakes her head slightly, as if saying no, but she answers me. "Okay, I'll admit I canceled a few doctors' appointments—so they weren't really able to keep track of how I was doing. I thought things were going just about the same, but obviously I wasn't the best judge of that."

Obviously. "But if you were still taking your pills, then how come—"

"My doctor here says that any severe stress could have triggered what happened—even though I was taking my

116

medicine. And I guess a *little thing* like having my marriage break up qualifies as severe stress," she adds with some of her old sarcasm. "I was already in quite a state, what with the fighting and everything last fall. Or maybe that's *why* we were fighting, I don't know."

"I thought I could make you better," I tell her, barely squeezing out the words.

"You can't make me better—and that's not your job, anyway. But you don't make me worse, either, you know." My mom looks at me searchingly, and she tiptoes her hand over to mine, which is lying on the grass. She covers my hand with hers and squeezes gently.

I love my mother's hand.

"But I tried so hard, Mom—shouldn't that count for something?"

"Darling, it counts for a whole lot," she says, "a *whole* lot. But I'm still sick, you know." She picks a few blades of grass and twiddles them between her fingers. "I'm always going to have my ups and downs, no matter how much medicine I take or how hard I try to get better." She sighs. "God, this is hard."

I have a hollow feeling in my chest by now, and my head is buried in my arms, which are resting on my knees.

Her, her, her. Nothing has changed.

Isn't she ever going to mention anything about giving poor Feather away?

Or ask what's been happening to *me*?

I can hear the sprinkler throbbing away like a heart-beat. I watch an ant climb up one side of a fallen leaf and down the other. "I know it's hard, Mom," I say.

I walk slowly toward the main building, where I'm sup-posed to meet my dad. It was hard saying good-bye to my mom—but I'll be back.

I'll be back, I'll be back.

Every so often during the past three weeks, it has been as though a flashlight was shining on my past, and I re-member some little thing that my mother said or did in the two months I took care of her. And I think, boy, was that nuts! Like the way I used to let her pick a fight with me every day for no reason, or those last couple of weeks when I would remind her about the dreaded mail—just to get her off my back.

I mean, I can see how she might have done such crazy things, her being sick and all, but she had *me* doing them, too. And they had started to seem almost normal, those things.

I didn't notice when that started to happen.

My mother was taking me with her across that invis-ible Sleeping Beauty bridge—and I didn't even know it. We were almost on the other side, though.

Right now, walking across Las Mariposas' blinding green lawn, it's as if I am halfway back across that bridge. I can see both what happened before my dad left last

December and what happened next. I can see the good parts about the crazy time with my mom—like being able to watch as much TV as I wanted, basically eating whatever I felt like eating, and having somebody who really, really needed me—and I can see the bad parts, too.

I try to explain to my father what those two months were like when he asks. I can only describe pieces of that time with my mom, though. The whole thing, and how normal and—and *good* it felt sometimes while it was happening, is something that I guess I'll have to keep to myself.

I know that it won't last forever, this seeing things from the middle of the bridge, this remembering. Pretty soon, I will forget.

But that's part of being real, too.

I think this bridge will lead me *away* from Lonely Island—and toward other people, no matter how worn out and strange they sometimes make me feel.

I think I'm finally heading in the right direction.

I can see my dad through the window in the swinging library door. He is the only one in the room, and he is sitting at a table, a stack of magazines at one elbow. "Hi," I say, pushing open the door.

He slams shut his copy of *InStyle* guiltily, as if he's been caught doing something naughty.

Reading menus from famous people's parties, I guess.

"Oh—there you are," he says, as if I'd wandered off without permission. "How's your mom?" he asks, getting up. He looks concerned—for *me*.

"She's good. She says hi."

Dad straightens his little pile of magazines, then gets up. "Let's go home," he says.

I'm in bed now, and I hear Dad coming up the stairs. He's leaving for Santa Barbara in the morning, and I'll go back to the Millers' house. I'm glad—I miss Stephanie. I pull the covers up tight.

There is a knock on the door, and Dad comes in to say good night. "How are you holding up?" he asks, perched on the edge of my bed like an oversized canary.

"Fine."

He is frowning, as if there is something serious he wants to say. I brace myself. "I—I feel really bad about what happened, Kara. About *everything*. It shouldn't have fallen on your shoulders the way it did."

"Well, I have pretty strong shoulders," I say, trying to joke.

"Not *that* strong," he says, and he smooths the bangs back from my forehead.

Almost the way Mom does.

It feels good.

"Is it all right if I go outside for a few minutes?" I ask Mrs.

Miller after dinner the next night. Stephanie is already in her bedroom doing her homework.

"Sure," Mrs. Miller says, looking a little concerned. "Do you want some company?"

"No thanks," I tell her. "I'm all right, really. I just want to walk around a little. I'll take Scarlett with me."

"Well, put on a sweater, honey."

"Okay." I grab a stretched-out old sweater from a hook near the back door, hoist a willing Scarlett over one shoulder, then slip outside. I walk past the Millers' dusty barbecue and onto the springy grass. It hasn't rained in a while, and no dew has fallen yet, so the grass is dry.

Mom is safe and sound at Las Mariposas, I think, settling cross-legged onto the grass with a warm and purring Scarlett.

Dad is in Santa Barbara, getting ready for me to move in with him. The orange velvet sofa bed awaits.

And I am in the Millers' backyard.

There are lots of people who care about me.

"Kara?" Stephanie's voice floats through the night from where she's standing by the kitchen door. "Mom said you were out here. Would you rather be alone?"

I think about this. *Would* I rather be alone? Part of me—the Lonely Island part—says yes, but the rest of me says no.

Stephanie knows how to be quiet.

"Come on out," I tell her.

We lie down on the cool dark grass. I stretch out my arms and legs and sink into the earth—or maybe the earth rises to catch me, I don't know.

I stare up at the night.

There is nothing between me and the stars, between me and the universe.

These are the same stars that were Karana's nightly companions for years on end, more than one hundred and fifty years ago. But not precisely the same, because no one else but me has ever lain on this exact same place on earth at this exact same time. No one else has seen these stars from this exact same perspective.

I am *here*. And I belong here—I'm absolutely part of the world.

I am real.

A few feet away, Stephanie plays quietly with Scarlett. I'm glad she came outside to be with me. I only wish I didn't have to leave Pasadena so soon.

It's strange, I think, wriggling a little on the scratchy grass, but when Karana was finally rescued from the island, she was taken to Santa Barbara—just the way I will be. It was too late for her to find the rest of her family, though. They had all moved away. Hardly anyone even spoke her language anymore, but at leasr she was able to tell her story to someone who *could* understand her. She lived out her final days at the mission.

God, I'll bet she was lonely.

She's even buried up there. Maybe my dad and I can look for the exact place together.

I wonder if Karana ever missed being all alone on her island?

I guess I'll find out.

Sally Warner is the author of many novels, including *Sort of Forever*, an ALA Quick Pick, a 1999 Best Book for the Teen Age, and a New York Public Library Best Book of 1998. She lives in Altadena, California, with her husband and a miniature wirehaired dachshund, Rocky.